P9-CDS-299
3 5674 05693114 1

6

Biblioteca Publica Bowen
3648 West Vernor
Detroit, Michigan 48216
313-481-1540

JUN 29 2018

THE WILD BOOK

written by
Juan Villoro

Translated from the Spanish by
LAWRENCE SCHIMEL

Illustrations by
EKO

Restless Books
for Young Readers

Copyright © 2017 Juan Villoro
Translation copyright © 2017 Lawrence Schimel

First published as *El libro salvaje* by Fondo de Cultura Económica,
Mexico City, 2008

All rights reserved.

No part of this book may be reproduced or transmitted without the prior
written permission of the publisher.

First Restless Books hardcover edition November 2017

Hardcover ISBN: 978-1-63206-147-8
Library of Congress Control Number: 2017944632

Cover design by Jori van der Linde
Interior illustrations by EKO
Text designed and set in Carré Noir by Tetragon, London

10 9 8 7 6 5 4 3 2 1

Restless Books, Inc.
232 3rd Street, Suite A111
Brooklyn, NY 11215

www.restlessbooks.com
publisher@restlessbooks.com
Printed in Canada

Contents

The Separation   3

The Vial of Iron   12

Uncle Tito   22

Books that Change Their Location   31

Remedies from the Pharmacy   47

Control Your Power   56

The Story a Book Tells Is Not Always the Same   66

The Shadow Books   73

The Wild Book   85

The Story Is Erased   98

An Enemy   111

The Pirate Book   121

The Prince Makes the Rules   132

Tito Cooks Novels   143

Catalina in the Library   153

Time and Cookies   163

Motors that Make no Noise   178

A Zigzag Radiation   189

The Shadow Club   200

Juicier Bait   212

What Starts When Something Ends   218

THE
WILD BOOK

The Separation

I'm going to describe what happened when I was thirteen. It's something I haven't been able to forget, as if the story had me by the throat. It might sound strange, but I can feel the hands of this story upon me, a sensation that's so specific I even know the hands are wearing gloves.

So long as the story is a secret, I am its prisoner. Now that I begin to write it, I feel a slight sensation of relief. The hands of this story are still on me, but one finger has loosened, like a promise that when I have finished I shall be free.

Everything began with the smell of mashed potatoes. My mother cooked mashed potatoes when she had something to complain about or was in a bad mood. She smashed the potatoes with more force than was necessary, with real fury. That helped her to relax. I've always liked mashed potatoes, even if in my house they tasted like problems.

That afternoon, as soon as I noticed the smell wafting from the kitchen, I went to see what was going on. My mother didn't notice my presence. She cried in silence. I would've done anything for her to once again be the smiling woman I adored, but I didn't know what might make her happy.

From then on, I heard her sobbing every night. I had taken to waking up at strange hours. As a child, I slept like a log, but at thirteen I began to have the scarlet dream—a nightmare that returned again and again. I found myself in a long hallway that was damp and dark. The flickering light of a flame came from the end of the hallway. I walked toward it and realized that I was inside a castle. My steps echoed in the darkness, making me aware that I was wearing iron boots. I was an armed soldier. I had to rescue someone at the end of the hallway who was crying. She had a woman's voice—a voice that was pleasant and incredibly sad. I walked toward that sound for an unnaturally long time, because the hallway seemed to lengthen with each step I took. Finally, I entered a room with red walls. My favorite color at that time was scarlet. How I liked the sound of the word "scarlet"! In the dream, I didn't see the crying woman, but I knew that she was there. Before speaking to her, I approached one of the walls, hypnotized by its scarlet color. Only then did I realize that its surface was liquid. No one had painted those walls. I placed my hands on the surface and the blood ran between my fingers. I always woke up at that moment, petrified with fear.

I turned on the light and looked at the map above the desk and at the only stuffed animal I sometimes still slept with. If someone had called me a child when I was thirteen, I would have been furious. I felt like a young man. My stuffed rabbit was there because I was fond of it. But I could sleep without him and I could defend myself on my own. Not even when I had the scarlet dream did I bring him into the bed. The rabbit watched me from his corner, with one eye lower than the other. I didn't ask him for help, but a long time passed before I could go back to sleep.

On the nights of the nightmare, I would wake up feeling very thirsty. If I had already drank the water my mother had placed on the nightstand, I didn't dare go into the kitchen to get some more, as if that were the location of the scarlet dream.

Then I would try to distract myself with the different countries on the map. My favorite was Australia, which was painted the color of bubble gum. My three favorite animals were Australian: the koala, the kangaroo, and the platypus.

What I liked most about koalas was how they hold on to trees. I would hug my pillow, just like a koala hugging a tree, until I'd fall asleep with the light still on.

Perhaps it was because I was growing up that I dreamed of these horrific things. My friends at school all liked stories about ghosts and vampires. I didn't like them, but I kept having that terrible dream.

One night I woke up even more frightened than usual. I turned on the lights and looked at my hands, afraid they would be stained with blood. But they only bore the ink stains they'd had when I came home from school. I looked at the map and, before I could even imagine distant countries, I heard a sob. It came from the hallway and had my mother's unmistakable tone.

This time I dared to leave my room and I walked barefoot to my parents' bedroom. Her grief was more important than my nightmare.

They slept in separate beds. The curtains were open and the moonlight entered the room and fell upon my father's bed, which was the one closest to the window. I've seen many beds since then, but none has affected me like this one did: my father wasn't there.

Mama cried with her eyes closed. She didn't realize that I was in the room. I went to my father's bed, pulled back the covers, and got in. I breathed in a delicious scent, of leather and lotion, and I fell asleep instantly. I never slept better than I did that night.

The next day, she didn't like finding me asleep there. I told her that I had sleepwalked and ended up there without realizing it.

"This is the last thing I need," Mama exclaimed. "A sleep-walking son!"

On the way to school, my sister, Carmen, made fun of me because I walked in my sleep. Then she asked me if I could teach her to sleepwalk. Carmen was ten and believed everything I told her. I explained to her that I belonged to a secret club that met at night; we wandered the streets without waking up.

"What is the club called?" Carmen asked me.

"The Shadow Club," I answered, the name coming to me suddenly.

"Can I join?"

"First you need to pass various tests. It's not so easy," I replied.

Carmen asked me to wake her up one night to take her to the Shadow Club. I promised that I would, but naturally I didn't.

Worried that I was walking in my sleep, Mama spoke to her friend Ruth, who had lived in Germany during World War II and had witnessed things that were more hair-raising than a somnambulant child. When she spoke on the phone to Ruth, Mama was soothed by these stories of things that were worse than her own troubles. Our life wasn't perfect, but at least we weren't being bombarded.

When I got back from school, Mama was talking on the phone with Ruth. However, once again, it smelled like mashed potatoes. Her friend's terrible stories hadn't managed to calm her down this time.

I left my backpack in my room. I went to the bathroom and then washed my hands (the annoying ink stains were still there). I went into the kitchen, following that wonderful smell that always heralded problems.

I stopped in the doorway and saw my mother crying in silence. Then I asked the question that I had been turning over and over in my head at school: "Where is Papa?"

She looked at me through her tears. She smiled as if I were a landscape, lovely and ruined.

"We need to talk," was her answer, but she didn't say anything else. She continued pounding the potatoes, then lit a cigarette, smoking haphazardly, so the ash fell into the food.

I remained standing there like a statue until she said:

"Your father is going to live outside the house for a while. He's rented a studio. He has a lot of work and we make too much noise. When he finishes all this work, he's going to Paris to build a bridge."

Something made me think that my father would never return to that bed beneath the moonlight.

Mama knelt down and hugged me. She'd never hugged me like this, kneeling on the floor.

"Nothing will happen to you, Juanito," she told me.

Every time she called me Juanito, something terrible happened. It wasn't an affectionate name, but a crisis name, the mashed potatoes of names.

I wasn't worried that something might happen to me, but rather that something might happen to her. I wanted her to be smiling like when she came to my school and I knew she was the prettiest of all the mothers.

"Don't worry," I answered, "I'm here with you."

It was the worst thing that I could have said to her. She cried more than ever, hugging me to her tightly for so long that the mashed potatoes with cigarette ash burned on the stove.

My sister arrived home later after piano lessons and she found us eating pizza. For her, the afternoon was lots of fun. Mama had no appetite and let Carmen eat as much as she wanted.

"I have something to tell you two," Mama said, chewing every word. "Papa went on a trip."

Carmen thought this was just grand, believing Papa would bring her back a stuffed toy as a souvenir.

I felt sad to see my sister happy because she didn't know the truth, but I would've done anything for her to never discover it.

Back then, divorce wasn't fashionable. None of my friends had divorced parents. However, I knew that it could happen. I had seen a very fun movie about a boy who had a great time because he had two homes and he managed to get everything he wanted in both of them.

My parents didn't fight but they also didn't speak as if they loved one another. They never kissed each other or held hands.

One afternoon, while looking through the papers on my father's desk, I found inside a book an envelope with wonderful drawings all across it: pink spirals, blue asterisks, zigzagging green lightning bolts. It looked like the cover of a rock album.

The envelope contained a letter. It was from a lady friend of Papa's who loved him very much and hoped to travel to Paris with him. I felt a hollow in the pit of my stomach and gave the letter to my mother.

That was two months before the mashed potatoes were burnt. Sometimes I thought it was my fault that Mama had become sad. Everything had happened because I gave her that terrible letter.

"Are you doing to get a divorce?" I asked Mama, when Carmen couldn't hear us.

I didn't want to have a good time in two homes like the boy in that movie. The truth is, I didn't want to see my father either. I just wanted things to go back to the way they were when my mother was content. Nothing more.

"I don't know what will happen. Papa loves you very much; that's what's important."

I didn't care if he loved me or not. I wanted him to love her. I went to my room to swear an important oath. I took the map and I swore by Australia we would be happy in that house, even if it took a lot of effort for me to achieve that.

That night I didn't have nightmares, but I also couldn't sleep.

I went to the room that had been my parents', where now there was one bed too many. Well, where I'd thought there was one bed too many. I was about to lie down when I saw that Carmen had beat me to it. As always, she seemed very content. Perhaps she dreamed they had let her into the Shadow Club.

The Vial of Iron

My mother began to leave cigarettes everywhere. She didn't even smoke them all the way. She was so nervous and made so many phone calls that the cigarettes piled up in the ashtray in little mountains without her having finished smoking a single one of them. There were smoke signals everywhere, as if we lived in an Indian camp.

Everything smelled of smoke and mashed potatoes. During the week of the separation, we ate meatballs with mashed potatoes from Monday through Saturday. On Sunday, my mother left us with her friend Ruth, who gave us some delicious German sausages, sprinkled with something I didn't recognize then: nutmeg.

Mama came to pick us up very late. Carmen was already asleep, hugging her stuffed beaver. I was about to collapse from exhaustion as well, but I managed to hear the conversation between her and her friend:

"The worst part is the summer holidays," my mother said. "I don't know what to do with them."

"Them" were Carmen and myself.

"Something will come up," Ruth said. "I can keep Pinta."

Pinta was our dog, a black-and-white Maltese. I was surprised, and somewhat relieved, that Ruth offered to have the dog stay with her and not us.

Why couldn't we spend the summer at home? There were two weeks until the end of classes. We barely studied anything at school anymore. The teacher had stopped being in a rush; he gave us each a sheet of paper to draw whatever we wanted, for hours on end. Then we sang very long songs, and it didn't matter if we made mistakes. It was as if our real classes were already over and we were just there out of obligation, filling up the days that remained until summer—the "long vacation," as we called it.

The best moment in life was the first day of vacation. The sun entered my bedroom differently: a lively sun, honey-colored, that warmed the curtains and announced that there were two months without school ahead. Anything could happen on that first day, as if the light were arriving all the way from Australia and its deserts of reddish sand.

If for an entire year you stop eating something you like a lot (chocolate or spaghetti or roast chicken) and then suddenly you try it again, you'll like it even more than before. That's what the first day of vacation was like.

Pablo, my best friend, lived two streets away from us. We had planned all sorts of games for the summer, even going into an abandoned house with broken windows where wild cats lived. It was going to be the best summer of my life. But Mama had other plans.

One afternoon I came back from playing with Pablo and found the hallway full of boxes.

"Your father's things," Mama explained.

I looked into one box and saw books. My fathered studied engineering and had written a book with a very strange title: *Bascule Bridges*. He explained to me once that they are bridges split into two parts that lift out of the way so boats can pass by.

I thought he would come for his things, but soon, two moving men showed up and took everything away in the blink of an eye.

"The things are going into storage until your father comes back from Paris."

"Wasn't he going to rent a studio?"

"He's going to build a bridge in Paris."

Perhaps he was going to build a bridge, but he was also going to see that lady friend who sent him that letter. I really liked the drawings she had made on the envelope, but I hated that my father went with her.

I also hated that my father might build a bridge there. It was no doubt one of those bridges that lifted out of the way so boats could pass by. That was his great specialty.

I preferred bridges that didn't separate and remained fixed, connected to both shores.

I didn't mind that all his boring books had been taken out of the house.

Mama took pills that were the same blue color as the sky for her headaches. Later we learned that she didn't simply have an ordinary pain, but suffered from something worse called a migraine.

She also suffered from gastritis. Orange juice was very harsh on her stomach, and she drank it through a glass straw so as not to gulp any air (which evidently made things worse). She was so pretty that she looked good even when she was drinking juice, even though she made a face as if she were drinking glass—crushed glass that tore her up from the inside.

Every third day she sent me to the pharmacy to buy her some remedy for her migraine or her gastritis.

Grandma told her, "It's from the cigarettes. Those cigarettes are the cause of everything."

But my mother couldn't stop smoking, at least not with so many problems weighing her down. Whenever my grandmother spoke of the evils of smoking, my mother closed one eye like a sharpshooter about to take a shot, lit a match with the quick movements of an expert marksman, and smoked with a special intensity. Then she spoke to us as if she were an Indian. From her mouth came smoke signals that meant, "I'll do whatever I feel like doing."

One night, I dreamed that I entered the abandoned house following a white cat. There were bonfires made from furniture everywhere. I reached the main living room, where a very large table was burning. Sitting at one sofa was my father, reading the newspaper. Suddenly, the newspaper began to burn, but he didn't do anything. He looked at the fire as if it were a news article. I woke up before the flames reached his hands.

Angrily, I thought my father would probably still prefer to live in an abandoned house, with burning furniture and newspapers, than to live with us. I got very mad at him and punched my pillow until I didn't have the strength to punch it anymore. Then I imagined being a koala and hugged my pillow as if it were my tree. I had cried, and the pillowcase was damp. Perhaps that's why I later dreamed that it rained a lot in the Australian forest where I led the life of a happy koala.

I loved to get into bed when the sheets were newly changed—the wonderful freshness of being there.

With the problems we'd been having since my father left, days and days would go by without my sheets being changed. At first I didn't realize, but one night I wondered if the sheets would ever again smell of fresh soap bubbles.

Carmen also noticed, and sprinkled some drops of shampoo on her sheets so they would smell like they were newly washed.

So no one could see she had been crying, my mother wore dark sunglasses. She looked like someone in the Mafia—especially when she wore a scarf around her head and had a cigarette in her mouth. But she looked good. Mafia women could be pretty.

There were only two days before vacation began when she told us for the second time, "We need to talk."

We went into the kitchen where she was peeling a melon. Lately she was so nervous that she cut herself when preparing anything. Every time she cooked, she brought out the first aid kit, certain she would injure herself. Then she put alcohol on the wound and that made the supper taste like a pharmacy.

I was afraid she would peel a finger while she spoke to us. Luckily, she put the knife down and said, "Pinta is going to spend the holidays with Ruth."

She spoke as if it were normal for dogs to go away for the summer.

"And what about us?" Carmen asked.

This part was harder for her. The words left her mouth as if they were made of cotton. "The Bermúdez family really loves you," Mama replied.

Leila Bermúdez was my sister's best friend. As always, Carmen was delighted by the solution. If she were on a boat about to capsize, she would find it a fun adventure to climb onto an inflatable raft. She finds something fantastic in even the worst of moments.

Since she was being sent to stay with her best friend, I thought I would be sent to Pablo's house. But Mama continued, "You are going to your Uncle Tito."

"Why?"

"He asked for you to come."

"I'd rather stay with Pablo. Or with Grandma."

"Pablo has four siblings. There's no room for you. And as for Grandma, she's too old to take care of another person."

"I'd rather go with someone else."

"Why?"

"Uncle Tito has white hairs sticking out of his nose," was the only thing I could think of.

It was true. My uncle shaved his ears, because he also had white hairs that grew there, but he didn't do anything about the hairs poking out of his nose.

"Your uncle loves you very much," Mama said.

That was also true. Every time I saw him, he read me a story from the thousands of books he had in his house. He was superb at talking about the life cycles of dragons, Middle Age swords, and the rocket ships of the future. But I didn't want to live with him. What was I going to do in a house as dark as his, filled with so many dusty books?

Uncle Tito had no children. He was my mother's cousin and had always lived alone, surrounded by his enormous library. Why had he asked for me to go live with him? He was nice enough, but I didn't need to see him that often.

"He has lots of wonderful books," Mama added.

"But no television set."

I liked television as much as I liked roast chicken. On the other hand, I wasn't much interested in books, especially if they were about engineering.

We didn't keep arguing, because she got very nervous, tried to cut another piece of melon, and a thin trickle of blood ran down the table.

"I can't even slice a melon," she said desperately.

We told her that wasn't true, that in the entire building there wasn't anyone who sliced melons as well as she did, and we didn't say anything more about where I would spend the summer holidays.

The next day I told myself that my mother loved me too much to send me to Uncle Tito's house. This couldn't be true.

It seemed right to me that Pinta went to Ruth's house to learn to bark in German, and that Carmen went to the house of Leila Bermúdez. I would stay with my mother. She needed me, of that I was sure.

The last day of classes, she forgot to pick us up. She often arrived very late and we were the last kids in the school yard, but this time she simply forgot to come for us. The janitor wanted to close the school gates because he was also starting his summer break.

I took Carmen's backpack and my own and told her that we would walk. I knew the way, but I had never taken it. It took us two hours to get home.

What could have happened for my mother to have forgotten to come get us? Had she died? Had she fainted? Did she have a migraine that no pill could cure?

We knocked on the apartment door and I told myself, "If it doesn't open in fifteen seconds, it's because she's dead."

The door opened in three seconds. Mama looked at us, quite surprised, as if we had stepped out of a dream. Only then did she realize she had forgotten to come get us.

"My god!" she said. "What time is it? Everything just slips out of my head these days!"

She begged us to forgive her a thousand different ways.

"I was packing your suitcases and I lost track of time," she explained to us.

Carmen's suitcase was ready, as was the basket with her favorite stuffed animals.

"Juanito is missing," my sister said, and she went to get the stuffed animal that had the same name as me (she had given him that name so that I would agree to bring her to the Shadow Club).

Even then I thought that Carmen would go somewhere else, but that I would remain. Mama couldn't bear to be away from me.

"Now I'll finish your suitcase," she said, and went into my room.

Slowly, I followed her.

I found her kneeling in front of my bed, folding shirts and carefully placing them in the suitcase. "She's doing this so that I think I'm going, but I won't fall for it," I thought.

She kept placing things in the suitcase until she came across a small, dark object. It was a tiny flask. The doctor had prescribed me iron. Every morning, I had to drink a spoonful of black syrup. It had a disgusting taste, but the pediatrician had said, "Iron is good for growth," as if I were some bridge being constructed. I hated that medicine everyone else thought was so good for me.

At that moment, seeing the vial of iron go into the suitcase, I knew it was all true—that I was leaving the house and would spend two long months with Uncle Tito. If my mother packed away something so specific and strange as that vial, it meant things were really serious.

At that moment I learned, for the first time and forever, that certain details make stories true. When the vial went into the suitcase, everything seemed real. I had to believe it: I was going to a house I barely knew.

What I couldn't know is that I was also going on the greatest adventure of my life.

Uncle Tito

My uncle lived in the old part of the city. In that neighborhood, some of the houses had been knocked down to construct modern buildings, others were about to fall apart all by themselves, and some had their balconies strapped firmly to their walls lest they drop off and split open the heads of passersby on the street.

It was in this area full of collapsing buildings, called the "Center," that one could find the house of my Uncle Ernesto, known as "Tito" by the family and as "Don Tito" by the messengers who brought him the books he ordered from different bookstores throughout the world.

My uncle lived with three cats: a black one named Obsidian; a white one named Ivory; and the son of both, my favorite, who was white with black spots and was named Domino.

For fifty-eight years, Uncle lived without any company other than his books and his cats. Suddenly, and much to the family's surprise, he decided one day that the time had come for him to contract matrimony.

He was married for one year to a woman of whom I remember only her round glasses and that she sneezed often because of all the dust on the books. In a moment of desperation, that lady told my uncle, "We can't live in this labyrinth; I'm allergic to old paper." Uncle bowed to her wishes: he left the house to his books and moved with his wife to a small apartment. But life without his library was very sad for him, so he decided to leave his wife and return to his books.

Because of all this, I was very surprised to be sent to his house. My uncle enjoyed his solitude; he didn't hold parties or even meetings, nor did he seem to need any company other than that of his three cats. Why had he wanted me to go there? It was all very strange.

In my suitcase, I brought with me one book: *All About Spiders*. I had already read it and I chose it precisely for that reason; I liked to reread a great book more than take a risk on an unknown one.

When we reached my uncle's house, I liked the head of a lion biting on a metal half-moon that served as a door knocker.

They were leveling the house next door and that made a lot of noise. Our knocks at his door with the lion's head could barely be heard. My mother asked me to kick the door, but since I wore rubber-soled shoes, I couldn't make a sound that could be heard over the nearby construction. For a moment, I had the hope that my uncle would never come and I could go home with my mother. Just then, the door opened.

"Have you been waiting long?" Uncle asked. "From inside, one can barely hear what goes on out here."

It was true. As soon as the large front door closed, there was a great silence, as if we were at the bottom of the sea.

"I've put in special insulation. It's the only way I can concentrate on my reading." Uncle Tito looked right at me, his eyes so attentive they seemed about to leap off his face.

I wanted to tell him, "Don't stare at me like that; I'm no book," but I didn't dare to.

There were bookshelves and books piled in columns that stretched up to the ceiling everywhere.

"Come into the living room," Uncle said.

The "living room" was a room that was slightly less congested. There were books on the walls but not on the chairs. We could sit ourselves at a table where a map served as a tablecloth. Australia was right in front of me. I couldn't help but mention that it was my favorite country.

"Splendid choice, my dear nephew," Uncle commented. "There isn't a lot of culture nor are there antiquities in that red desert, but it's the home of the platypus, the most

fabulous of animals—a biological summary, an encyclope-
dia of what it might be without quite being it; the platypus
could be a duck, a beaver, or a marmot. Its secret lies in
disguising itself as other animals in order to be itself. A
great character actor."

I didn't understand anything he said. Had Uncle gone
cuckoo since we'd last seen him?

Then he added, with much enthusiasm, "What's more,
Australia has the best ocean waves—not so much for their
shape, but because they bathe the Australian female, a
species superior even to the platypus. Somewhere I have
a calendar of Australian females in bikinis."

My mother looked at Uncle with concern and took my
hand. She seemed to regret having brought me here. My
uncle's strange words began to interest me.

"Would you like a smoked tea?" he asked, and left the
room before we could respond.

"Will you be all right here, Juanito?" My mother caressed
my hair and looked at me with sad eyes.

She had told me that she needed a few weeks alone in
order to look for a smaller apartment, now that we were
only three. I didn't want to worry her any more than she
already was by telling her I thought Uncle was half-mad.
Interesting, but mad.

In a corner of the room I saw a silvered cobweb in the
shape of a triangle, identical to an illustration in my book
All About Spiders.

"I like this house," I answered.

"If you miss me, you can call me."

This wasn't so easy. For my uncle, the phone was an error of modern life. He hated for its ringing to interrupt his reading. "I don't want to hear any other voice than my own conscience," he said when someone asked him why he didn't have a telephone.

"At the pharmacy across the street there's a pay phone," my mother explained. "Here," she said, giving me a little bag full of coins to pay for the calls.

Uncle returned with a steaming teapot.

"Those journeys by boat were not in vain," he said. "Thanks to the daring crews who reached as far as India and Ceylon, and their captains' wonderful habit of drinking tea, today we can soak these leaves in hot water. Smell, my dear family members. Would you like some smoked tea?"

Uncle Tito served us before we had a chance to answer. The tea really did smell like smoke.

"'Lap-sang Soo-shong,' that's what this rich variety is called."

"Is it good for children?"

"Well, I would say that Juan is no longer a child," my uncle opined, and I liked him better.

We drank the curious tea until my mother said she needed to speak to Tito alone.

My uncle proposed that I take a look around the house while they spoke. He handed me a little bell. "If you get lost," he explained, "shake the bell and I shall come to your aid."

Was it possible to get lost inside a house? Very soon I discovered that it was, and how it might happen.

I walked down a hallway lined with bookcases and entered the first room I came to. The room was two stories tall, covered with books from wall to wall, with a balcony halfway up that could be accessed through a set of stairs, letting one reach the books on the second level.

I wandered into another room, not seeing anything but books. Suddenly, Domino leaped from a shelf and slipped through a doorway. I followed him and found myself in a dark corridor. I tried to find the light switch, but my hands encountered only books bound in leather. I tripped on some books that were on the floor. I again searched for the light switch and, thinking I had found it, pulled down on a small lever. A trapdoor opened below my feet and I fell down a slide until I reached a mountain of sheets, in which there were also a few books. Luckily, I hadn't lost the little bell. I shook it with all my might until my uncle came.

"What are you doing in the laundry room, Nephew?" he asked me, surprised.

"I fell from up there."

"You'll get used to the house. It has lots of nooks and crannies, but it's rather practical. You've already discovered where the dirty clothes go."

"There are some books here."

"They're to be dried and ironed. Sometimes I spill tea on the pages."

When we returned to the living room, my mother looked very serene. It had done her good to speak with my uncle.

"We've already seen how useful the bell is," Tito said. "Don't ever lose track of it. I suggest you tie it to you very securely. I have a book about knots and I would recommend one called Margarita; once tied, not even God can undo it," he recited.

My mother said goodbye with lots of hugs and kisses. I smelled her hair, the best smell in the world.

She reminded me to call her now and then from the pharmacy across the street.

When my uncle and I were alone, he said, "Very good. Now I suggest we put into practice the method of the famous detective Sherlock Holmes to get to know people: we shall speak of our defects. What are the worst faults that you have, Nephew?"

"I don't know."

"To live with someone, you need to know what problems they might create for you. Nobody is perfect. If you accept yourself, you'll get along well."

"I can't think of anything."

"Are you perhaps a bit conceited? We all have our little defects. That's fine. I shall begin." He paused, took a long sip of his tea, and began to list his defects. "One: I snore at night, but this isn't a problem because you'll have your own room; two: I don't like for people to talk to me when I am reading; three: I can't stand for anyone to sing; four: I get very upset about things that are not important, but I get over my anger very quickly; five: I am horrible at numbers and keep change that belongs to other people . . . "

This last made me worry for my bag of coins to speak on the telephone at the pharmacy. I would need to hide it very well.

"Now it's your turn," my uncle insisted.

"Sometimes I have nightmares and I shout at night," I answered. "I also get cramps in my legs; I am not very neat and I leave my clothes on the floor; I don't wash my hands very well and sometimes they're sticky; I get distracted when I am thinking and I don't pay attention to what people are saying to me; I am clumsy and I break things . . . "

I had never realized I had so many defects, but it was good for me to say them out loud.

"I can live with all that," my uncle stated thoughtfully. "And you? Can you live with mine?"

"Yes."

"Perfect. Those problems will bring us close together."

My uncle gave me a hug and, in doing so, knocked over his cup of tea. Some droplets fell onto his pants.

"Darn it!" he shouted, furious; then he watched me. "See? I get very angry over things that don't matter. But I get over it in the blink of an eye. The problems that really matter catch my attention, but they don't worry me. I have read enough books for it to be this way; authors have shown me that the great problems are interesting."

"Do you like spiders, Uncle?" I asked.

"Why do you ask?"

I pointed to the triangular spiderweb in the corner of the room.

"In this house there are inoffensive spiders that protect us from the mosquitoes. Have you tried to read while a mosquito is buzzing in your ear? I loathe mosquitoes—they are orchestras of desperation. They buzz and buzz and you can't think of anything else. On the other hand, spiders are friends of silence; they devour the mosquitoes with all their hullabaloo."

"I brought a book with me called *All About Spiders*," I mentioned.

"This is the right place to study the nonvenomous species."

Uncle Tito placed a hand on my shoulder and added, "You're going to have a good time here, Nephew." Then he took a deep breath, like a swimmer about to dive into the water. "We are going to have a good time. This house needs a young brain. Your wits are welcome."

And that's how my time in the labyrinth of books began.

Books that Change
Their Location

My Uncle Tito assigned me a pleasant room, with a view of a small garden. In the morning, I heard birdsong and I felt like I was out in the country. I slept very well. I didn't have any cramps and I didn't dream about the terrible scarlet room.

Around eight I heard noises and decided to go down for breakfast. I was hungry enough to eat five biscuits. Would Uncle let me eat that many? My mother said that my jelly sandwiches were making my belly chubby.

I took the little bell that I had left on the nightstand and traveled through the hallways, orienting myself by the sound of plates that (I thought) came from the dining room.

Thus I reached a room where I found a heavyset woman who had her back to me.

"Good morning!" I said to her.

"Oh, my stars and garters!" she shouted, and dropped the plates she held in her hand. These shattered on the wooden floor. "Who are you?" she asked. "Are you a ghost? No, ghosts don't wear slippers." And she pointed at mine with a finger that was as thick as a sausage.

"I'm Juan, Tito's nephew."

"I'm Eufrosia. Mister Tito didn't tell me you were coming. He's got his head in the clouds, always lost in his books. He's a cloud with pants. What do you want for breakfast? A Homer omelet, Aristophanes porridge, Five Muse muesli, or an Isabelline sandwich?"

Everything sounded really strange. I asked what the Homer omelet was like.

"It's made with the freshest eggs and with one's eyes closed. Then you add a bit of Greek cheese, and it's served dripping in olive oil."

My mouth started to water.

I ate in the kitchen because the chairs in the dining room were all covered in books. The omelet was even yummier than its description. I decided to eat one every day. When I like something I like to repeat it, never growing tired of it. Mama thinks it's absurd to always order the same pizza, but if my favorite is a salami pizza, why should I order a different kind?

"Why do you have to make the omelet with your eyes closed?" I asked Eufrosia.

"Mister Tito told me that it was invented by Homer, a blind genius. We close our eyes out of respect for him. Did you know that your uncle's father was also blind?"

I didn't know that or I hadn't remembered. But we didn't keep talking about the subject because a voice behind me said, "How early you wake up, champion!"

Uncle wore a green felt sleeping cap. He poured himself tea into a soup bowl and slurped the liquid with lots of noise.

"I forgot to tell you about another of my defects: I can't eat in silence. I chew too loudly. I don't like food unless I can hear it. Books ask for silence, but a good mouthful should resound, even if just a little. Have you met Eufrosia? She's the cook, the laundress, and a specialist in removing crumbs but not touching spiderwebs."

"Pleased to meet you," the friendly woman told me, as if she were just seeing me for the first time.

"Eufrosia doesn't live in the house," Uncle Tito explained. "She comes in with the trills of the early birds and leaves when it gets dark. At night, only you and I and a million books live here."

"Are there really that many?" I asked.

"The truth is that I've never been able to count them. Books are very slippery. You look for one on the shelf and you find it on another, or you don't find it for years and suddenly it appears right in front of your nose. At first I thought Eufrosia moved them from one place to another when she dusted, then I thought that I was the one who moved them without realizing it. I'm very distracted—anyone can see that. But then I came to the conclusion that the books move around on their own—they search you out or flee from you." Uncle took a long sip of tea. "You'll think that this is an absurd idea, but I've verified it time after time. I'll give you an example, to see if we understand one another. No scientist has been able to know why some socks disappear. You put two into the wash and suddenly only one comes out. The other has vanished into thin air. It is not a question of theft—who would be able to use just one sock? Something similar happens with books. When you bring too many of them together, it's difficult for them to remain still. Books search for their own arrangement. Sometimes they want to be read, and other times to not be read."

I wanted Uncle to keep talking about this subject, but he twisted his lips in a strange way and said, "I've got to use the facilities. Tea is a diuretic."

"What does 'diuretic' mean?"

"That you have an urgency to urinate. If you drink one cup of tea but then urinate a whole jug's worth, then you had a diuretic drink."

Thus I learned about another of Uncle's habits. No conversation lasted long because he rushed off to the bathroom every short while.

When he returned I asked him, "It wouldn't be because you're drinking too much tea?"

"Of course not! Tea clears the ideas and cleans the kidneys. It is wonderful to urinate. Don't you like it when you pee for a really long time? I've managed to urinate for three minutes straight. I timed it with a cyclist's stopwatch."

"I like to urinate, if I feel the need to," I answered.

"Logical response, even if not very enthusiastic. Sometimes it's necessary to exaggerate, Nephew. One must make the possibilities of life even larger; urinating for three minutes is more fun than urinating for ten seconds."

Afterwards, Uncle Tito showed me some of the sections of his enormous library. As we wandered the house, Ivory and Obsidian followed us at a discreet distance. Domino, on the other hand, climbed up onto the shelves and sometimes knocked down a book. Perhaps he was responsible for the books' changing location.

Uncle oriented himself without difficulty in those rooms whose sizes were impossible to calculate. From one room you moved into another, and suddenly you found yourself in an inner courtyard with a glass roof. The books didn't merely occupy all the walls, they also formed a labyrinth inside each room, making movement through them even more difficult. From one wall you could never see the wall across from it—there were too many books in the way!

The library had been ordered into sections, following a rather strange system. Signs with red lettering indicated what the books in that area were about, but the subjects were quite random. On that first exploration, I copied down the following signs into a notebook: "Cheeses That Stink But Taste Delicious," "Small Dogs," "The Bengal Tiger," "Maps of the Ancient World," "The Teeth of Grandmothers," "Swords, Knives, and Lances," "Foolish Atoms," "Motors That Make No Noise," "Orange Juice," "Things That Look Like Mice," "Black Books," "How to Exit the Labyrinth," "Marmalade Is Not Money," "Carnivorous Flowers," "The Fisherman and His Hook," "Aviation Accidents," "Rockets That Don't Return," "Explorers Who Never Set Out," "The Meaning of Silence," "Attack Soccer," "1001 Spaghetti Sauces," and "How to Govern Without Being President."

Those sounded like the titles of random books; however, they were the names of sections which, in a very strange way, brought together different books. For example, the section "Explorers Who Never Set Out" contained seventy-two volumes related to this curious subject.

It seemed my relative had books about the most diverse topics. I asked him if he had bought any books that dealt with koalas.

"They should be among the books about bears," he answered. "I don't know how many there are. I stopped counting when I reached the number five hundred."

"And have you read all of them?"

"Of course not. A library is not to be read completely, but to be consulted. Here there are books which are around just in case. I have read all my life, but there are many things about which I know nothing. What's important is not to have everything in one's head but to know where to find it. The difference between someone who's vain and someone who's wise is that the vain man only appreciates what he already knows, and the wise man searches for what he doesn't yet know."

That afternoon, someone called at the front door. Uncle paid for a package he had been sent and made a muddle of the addition and subtraction. Suddenly he said to me, "I need your brains, Nephew ... How much is one hundred less fifty-eight?"

"Forty-two."

"Excellent idea!"

"It's not an idea, Uncle, it's a result."

"Sorry, I am a bit befuddled."

Uncle had received something that left him quite overwrought.

"My nerves make me forget the things I learned when I was your age," he said.

"Why are you nervous?"

"You don't know how difficult it is to get ahold of this book."

We went into the kitchen, where he took a knife, cut the cord that bound the package, tore away the brown wrapping paper, and showed me a very old book with a dark blue cover. It looked as if it were bound in whale skin. Uncle opened it. It was written in a language I didn't understand.

"What's it about?" I asked.

"Actually, it's not about anything. This book serves to find other books. It's an explorer book."

"I don't understand."

"Let me go urinate, then I'll brew a pot of my smoky tea and I'll tell you everything," Uncle said.

After he had done all these things, he placed a hand upon the book with the blue cover and explained, "Some centuries ago a science was invented for everything that has to do with books."

"Is it a science to find lost books?"

"To a certain degree, my dear detective, but not exactly."

"What is it, then?"

"It's a science to understand how books behave and where they might go. Nobody has so much character as a book. A library is a collection of souls, Nephew. Books move like the souls in cemeteries, to approach someone or to flee before them."

"Your library has ghosts?"

"Not so fast, Nephew. Over the course of many happy years, I've learned that every book has a spirit. That spirit searches for its reader—its favorite, ideal, absolute reader." His eyes shone with a rare delight.

I looked at the hairs that poked out from my uncle's nostrils and the white mane of hair that fell all disordered down his back. His bulging eyes stared at me intensely, as if I were an insect under a magnifying glass. I am ashamed to say it, but right then I thought he was quite mad.

"The books move around by themselves?" I asked him.

"I thought we had already clarified that point. Haven't you ever had it happen that you put a notebook down in one place and then you find it somewhere else?"

"That happens because you forget where you put it down."

"Secrets are not that simple. I've lived long enough to know that books change their location of their own volition. The question is, why do they do so? That's what this book is about, written in Latin in the fifteenth century, when only the wise and a few monks spoke that dead tongue."

At that moment, Eufrosia arrived with a cake that smelled delicious.

"Newton pie!" Uncle exclaimed, happy with life. "Look, Nephew, it's covered in crunchy bumps, in memory of the apple that fell on Newton's head and thanks to which he discovered the law of gravity. I suppose you already know that, since you're so clever and already know the number forty-two so well. The pie is filled with apples, which help in one's digestion and prove the law of gravity; everything winds up dropping down, my dear Nephew. First you eat, then you go to the bathroom."

It seemed terrible to me that someone so interested in books would make scatological jokes like a little child. Uncle Tito really acted like a loon.

While we ate the delicious pie, my relative scattered crumbs everywhere. I had never seen anyone eat with such enthusiasm and such clumsiness. Eufrosia returned a short while later with a vacuum cleaner.

Since Uncle hates noise, except for that which he makes himself when he chews, he covered his ears for a while and we couldn't keep chatting.

Unlike Uncle, Eufrosia loved to hear sounds. For example, the noise of the vacuum didn't stop her from hearing the front doorbell. She went to see who it was and returned with a letter.

"Express mail," she announced, and, to my surprise, added, "and it's for you."

When the mail arrived at home, I always hoped there was a letter for me, but the letters were always for my father. Now, for the first time, I received a letter. It had a stamp that showed Napoleon from the times when he was a young soldier and had long hair.

The envelope contained a postcard. One side had an image of the Eiffel Tower and on the back, my father's chicken-scratch writing and his signature like twisted wires.

The postcard read:

Beloved son,

I know that these are difficult times for you, but I will always love you. I am in the middle of constructing a very big bridge. When I'm through, I'll come back and we'll go to the zoo and to a soccer match.

I love you,
Papa

Right then I didn't want to go to the zoo or to watch a soccer match.

I was about to tear up the postcard. The Eiffel Tower reminded me of the iron that I should take, which tasted terrible. Eufrosia had turned off the vacuum and Uncle was looking at me curiously. I was ashamed to be upset. I couldn't just tear up the postcard as if I were a lunatic in some film. To calm down, I asked Uncle to keep talking about the books that change location on their own.

"That's precisely the subject I wished to return to," he said, with much enthusiasm. "There are two ways that a book might come to you: the normal way and the secret way. The normal way is that you purchase it, or someone lends it to you or gives it to you. The secret way is much more important; in that case, it is the book that chooses its reader. Sometimes the two ways get mixed up together. You think you decided to buy a book, but in reality, the book put itself there for you to see it and be drawn to it. Books don't want to be read by just *anyone*, they want to be read by the best people—that's why they search out their readers. Let's go get a breath of fresh air."

41

I thought we would go out into the garden that surrounded the house, but that's not what we did. For my uncle, "fresh air" meant moving to a place with fewer books than usual. We went to one of the many large rooms that made the house strange, which I couldn't have found without getting lost. It was a room full of rugs with complicated designs (like intertwined serpents) and potted ferns, which got sun from a skylight. There were only books on a desk and on the coffee table.

I had the strange sensation of having been here before. That's why I was so surprised when Uncle Tito said, "Ten years ago, when you were barely two years old, you were in here. Your parents left you with me for a few hours because they had to take care of some things in this part of town. You behaved well, I won't say you didn't. You played for a while with a little fire engine and then fell asleep. Your parents came for you and everything seemed like an ordinary, everyday visit. I'm very distracted, as you know, and it took me a while to realize that something had happened."

"What happened?"

"I need to go to the bathroom."

"Hold it in, Uncle, you can't stop the story here."

"I'll tell you everything very quickly. After your visit, many books moved around. Nothing like this had ever happened to me before. You woke up the souls of the library. You have a rare power. You are a Lector Princeps."

"A Lector Princeps?"

"A unique reader. In normal life you're my nephew Juan, friendly and with a bit of a belly. For the books you are a prince. That's why I needed you here. Now I am going to the bathroom."

Uncle left the room quite hurriedly. I looked at the ferns and they seemed like fabulous plants to me, like a miniature jungle. Were there spiders in there? The ambience suggested something strange. Uncle returned a few minutes later.

"This library needs you, Nephew," he said, emphatically. "You don't know how difficult it was for me to convince your mother for you to come here. I've been begging her for years. She thinks I am half-crazy." He paused, as if carefully calculating what he wanted to say. "The truth is that I'm not normal, but who wants to be as common as a dishrag? Worthwhile people are distinguished for something special or unique."

I realized all the coincidences that had made it possible for me to be there. After my father left, my mother needed to be alone in order to take care of things and finally gave in to Uncle's begging for me to visit him.

His eyes shone more than ever when he said, "Every time you've visited this house, the books have felt your presence." That made me feel a bit afraid, until he added, "I don't know what kind of Lector Princeps you are. We'll have to discover that."

"Have the books moved since I've arrived?"

"That's what's strange. On this occasion, they're extremely quiet, as if they've been preparing something. I guess they know that you live here, and they don't wish to act rashly."

"You speak of them as if they were people."

"They're more than that—they're *super*people. They live forever, searching for readers."

I didn't want to disillusion my uncle, but I also didn't want to give him false hope, so I suggested, "Perhaps I no longer attract the books."

"That could happen, of course. There are wonderful children who grow up to be idiots and the books stop being interested in them. I don't mean you, of course. I think that the books are studying you."

"I like to read, but not too much," I added. "I prefer to watch television, to ride my bike, or to play with my dog, Pinta, or with my friend Pablo."

"It doesn't matter; the books feel that you can read them better than other people can. A Lector Princeps isn't someone who reads more books but a person who finds more in what they do read."

"Am I really a Lector Princeps?"

"You have all the characteristics, starting with your ears, because they get hot when you read. That's a sign of concentration."

"How do you know my ears get hot?"

"I took the precaution of touching them while you read your book about spiders. To a certain degree, I am glad that your mother has delayed in accepting my invitation. Now you're thirteen years old and you better understand what you read. We'll see if the books still consider you to be one of theirs. Sometimes there are Lector Princeps Interruptus. Occasionally, someone is born with enormous capacity for reading, but life turns them into cretins. There are famous imbeciles who were very refined babies."

"Are there various kinds of Lector Princeps?"

"Yes, many. I'd be content if you were a Princeps Continuum."

"Which kind is that?"

Uncle seemed a bit desperate. "As its name indicates, Nephew of mine with cork for brains, the Princeps Continuum is the kind that keeps the talent for reading over the course of their lifetime."

"And there are other kinds of readers?"

"Yes, there are others, but let's not be too ambitious—it won't do for you to know too much. It's enough for you to help me to find the book that I have never been able to read."

"Is it here in your house?"

"Yes. I had it in my hands and I've not been able to recover it."

"And did you already read it?"

"No one has read it. It is a unique case."

"Not even its author read it?"

"It doesn't seem to have an author. I tell you, it's unique."

"Do you know at least what it's about?"

"I can't tell you."

"What's it called?"

"I don't want to tell you."

"Why? That could help me find it."

"That would help you find it in a normal way. I want you to find it in a secret way. If you deserve the book, it will come to you. That's what I want you to help me with during your two months of summer vacation."

Remedies from the Pharmacy

I was surprised that my uncle, having read so many books, was unable to add or subtract.

"Look," he explained unenthusiastically to me. "An educated man isn't a know-it-all. I am dreadful at math, sports, fixing machinery, driving vehicles, and looking for yogurt cups in the fridge; I won't even get into geography, which I've never been good at. If you left me in Africa and asked me to go to Russia, I'd wind up in Toluca. The only map I know is the one for this house and that's enough for me."

His way of approaching knowledge seemed so strange to me that I asked him, "Did you go to school?"

"I studied in a normal and boring way until I was fourteen years old, then my father gave me this library as a legacy and I started to read in a disordered fashion. I was never a good student; being forced to study makes me despair."

"Me, too," I told him.

"Of course, I have a lot of respect for the things I don't know. In this library there are magnificent books on subjects I'm not interested in. I don't like the army and wars make me vomit green. However, it is necessary for them to be studied. If someone wants to know what man has done to strap on their swords or fly through the air with explosives, I can consult my sections: 'Great Generals,' 'Death Strategies,' 'Lightning-fast Wars,' 'Winter Invasions of Russia,' 'Battles that Ended in a Draw,' 'Heroic Losers,' and 'Victors Who Fled,' among others I can't recall just now."

"If you are so bad at math, how do you add things up?"

"This house has forty basic digits: mine and Eufrosia's, counting both fingers and toes. That can take care of the most urgent adding and subtracting. When things get more scientific, we go out into the street and ask someone to lend us their fingers or to do the math for us. In really terrible cases, I ask the director of the Math Department at the university, who is a very good friend of mine. Once I asked him to check over the supermarket accounts and he was surprised that broccoli was so expensive. He has a friend who sells it at half the price, a famous inventor who lives on a ranch or something like that. But I've lost myself, what were we talking about?"

"You said that a wise man didn't need to know everything."

"Indeed. I already told you that every book chooses its reader. I, for example, have never been sought out by books with numbers or chemical formulae. If I had to score myself, I would assign myself the following:

MATHEMATICS: zero.

PHYSICS: two.

CHEMISTRY: zero.

GEOGRAPHY: one, and the only reason I don't give myself a zero is because I know the geography of my own house.

HISTORY: eight.

SPORTS: zero.

MYTHOLOGY AND STORIES OF IMAGINARY HEROES: ten.

LANGUAGES: ten.

GOSSIP ABOUT FAMOUS PEOPLE: ten.

SPELLING: seven."

Uncle Tito's relationship with knowledge was very extreme; he knew a lot about some things and nothing about others.

"Do you know what man's real problem is?" His eyes, big and round as ping-pong balls, came close to my own.

He didn't tell me because once more he felt like he had to urinate.

When he returned, I had to remind him of what we had been talking about.

"Oh, yes. Man has all kinds of problems, but there is one that interests me particularly: not knowing how to measure oneself. A tailor can measure a person on the outside without any trouble, but we have a hard time measuring ourselves on the inside. We need an inner tailor." He stuck a pencil in his ear and scratched himself energetically, then continued talking. "Grades are like the menu in a restaurant. Math appeals to me as little as creamed carrots. I deserve a zero in that subject. As you can see, there are some things I am not so bad at: I know lots about myths and legends, enough about history, and I speak twelve languages, including living ones, dead ones, and ailing ones (such as the dialect full of curses that the police in this city use). But that doesn't say much. The true qualifications of an intelligent person should be these:

ABILITY TO CONNECT ONE IDEA WITH ANOTHER: ten.
ABILITY TO SUMMARIZE WHAT HAS BEEN LEARNED: ten.
ABILITY TO THINK FOR YOURSELF WHAT SOMEONE ELSE KNOWS: ten."

Uncle waited for a response. Since I didn't say anything, he added, "The mind is a machine for thinking. What is most important is not to flood it with data, but to learn how to use it. Every head is a different machine, so every person needs to use their own method for thinking."

Uncle Tito left me a bit dizzy with all this talk about scores. I was neither a very good nor a very bad student. I liked some subjects more than others, but I didn't understand very well what "thinking for myself" meant. What a tangled mess this business of being wise seemed to be!

I missed my friend Pablo. Instead of spending my break with him exploring the mysteries of an abandoned house, I had to listen to my uncle's strange ramblings.

And for the first time in some days I missed my father. I was still mad at him because he had left, but I remembered the buildings and bridges that he had helped me make with plastic blocks. He was excellent at that. When I saw his large and precise hands, able to put together an entire miniature city, I felt content and safe. In his hands, the most complicated towers seemed easy to make. My dad never asked strange questions like Uncle Tito did; he just helped me play. They were two very different ways of being. Now that I was with my uncle, I missed the benefits of someone as practical and quiet as my father.

I wanted to rest a bit after this long conversation and asked for permission to go to the pharmacy and talk on the phone.

"Perfect," Uncle said. "And while you're there, buy me some aspirin. An idea has been gnawing at me for two days now."

It was good for me to go out onto the street, to hear noises, see cars, but it was especially good for me to go into the pharmacy.

I had always liked the smell of rubbing alcohol, soaps, and cough syrups that pharmacies have. I breathed in the scent of the remedies and, in the back, between a million boxes with the strange names of medicines, I saw a pair of eyes that caught my attention. I also saw a nose and some hair. I'd seen other pretty girls, but this one made me feel butterflies in my stomach. My throat closed up, as if I'd swallowed dust.

I loved that she wore a white lab coat. It fit her perfectly; it didn't belong to her mother or some older sister. It was tailored precisely to her size, with her name sewn on one pocket: Catalina.

An old man had arrived before me. He ordered ten different medicines.

Catalina turned and found them with no difficulty. She moved easily among the boxes and vials lined up by type.

Compared to the order of the pharmacy, my uncle's library represented absolute chaos. Being there was like looking at a calm pond after emerging from a torrential storm.

The old man paid with a large bill. Catalina pulled out a calculator and her fingers flew over the keys with great speed.

She handed over the change and then looked at me with her honey-colored eyes.

"What can I get for you, sir?" she asked me.

No girl had ever called me "sir" before.

I didn't answer and, I'm sure, turned red from nerves.

She smiled and I saw she had one tooth that was slightly crooked. This minimal defect made her even more lovely, since it made her different from any other girl.

She asked me again what she could get for me.

Until that moment I had thought I knew what a lovely woman should look like. What I didn't know, and what Catalina showed me, was that someone could be lovely in such a detailed and particular way. Seeing her, I liked things that I never knew I could like before; for example, her thin fingers and the way she picked things up.

I discovered that a flask of medicine could be picked up in a lovely way.

My head was spinning.

I couldn't speak. I had fallen in love. I had fallen in love at "sir."

"Are you mute?" my beloved asked, with calm interest.

Used to seeing people suffering from all sorts of ailments, this girl was ready to treat any client quite naturally.

I breathed in the air of the pharmacy and I knew that all medications I took in my lifetime were going to remind me of the moment when Catalina looked at me with such intensity, and asked, "Do you speak Spanish?"

I nodded and gulped loudly, almost as if I had swallowed a coin.

She went and got a small round metal tin. She took out a red tablet and told me, "For your throat."

I sucked on the tablet and she said, "That's better. Can you talk now?"

I couldn't. I had fallen in love again, this time because she'd stopped using "sir."

"Catalina!" someone shouted from the back of the pharmacy.

"I'll be right back," she said.

She returned a short while later, carrying enough packages of gauze wraps to make a mummy happy.

Uncle Tito had said that a wise man is someone who thinks for himself. In front of Catalina, I couldn't think at all. Everything flew out of my head, as if I were a blank sheet of paper.

"Did the cat swallow your tongue?" she asked.

The throat lozenge she'd given me sunk down to the bottom of my stomach. I wanted to sink into the very center of the Earth myself, but a miracle allowed me to say, "I want aspirin."

"Nothing more?" she asked, as if the request left her wanting.

"And something for growing pains."

"Where does it hurt?" she asked, looking concerned.

Catalina was worried about me! I tried to explain to her that sometimes I woke at night from the terrible pain in my legs.

"That's normal," she said. "You're growing. You're going to be very tall," she added. "Do you take vitamins?"

"I take iron," I told her, and suddenly I realized that I hadn't taken it since I arrived at my uncle's house.

"Iron tastes like a cooking pan," she said authoritatively. "I wouldn't recommend it."

Right after, she handed me a cellophane bag with anise drops inside.

"Will this alleviate growing pains?" I asked her.

"No, but it will take away the sour taste of the iron," Catalina told me.

She also recommended I use a cream with a fantastic name I've never seen again: *Frotasín*. Then she explained that I should apply it with a circular rubbing motion (her hand made tiny little circles).

I paid and she gave me the change with experienced hands, used to distinguishing the value of the coins by touch.

To my surprise, she then said, "I saw you coming out of the house across the street. Do you live there?"

"Yes, with my uncle."

"They say he has lots of books. Can you loan me one? I get bored when nobody comes into the pharmacy."

"Which book?"

"You choose."

I left feeling so happy that I didn't realize I hadn't made my phone call.

I only remembered when my uncle asked me, "How is your mother?"

"Fine, I guess."

"Didn't you speak with her?"

I didn't answer. I walked past him toward my uncle's books, hoping to find one that Catalina would like.

Control Your Power

Eufrosia's cooking was excellent. In the afternoons, she left me a sandwich and a glass of chocolate milk in front of the fireplace. I loved eating this snack while watching the logs burn. According to my uncle, the tasty sandwich was made with wild boar ham. It seemed a bit strange for that to be true, but it did taste unlike anything I had ever tried before: it was better than a super-sausage and more delicious than a fine salami. Perhaps it was true that I ate wild boar ham on those afternoons.

At night, we had crispy chicken for dinner or spaghetti with a sauce that must have had tomatoes in it, because it was red, but was also enriched with fine herbs that gave it a surprising, exquisite taste.

Curiously, although I ate much more and much better than I did at home, I was getting skinnier.

"It's because of the library," my uncle explained to me. "This is a place for great walkers."

That was true. Every day, I traveled never-ending hallways. Since they kept twisting and turning, it was impossible to know how long they were. By midafternoon, when I usually had a snack, my feet were numb.

A few times I was rescued by Uncle Tito on those walks that seemed to have no end. One book led me to another, and suddenly I found myself in an unfamiliar place, dying of hunger or desperate to use the toilet. Then I shook the little bell he had given me.

Sometimes long minutes passed before my uncle found me. When he was very busy with his reading, he asked Eufrosia to come for me instead. She walked very slowly and the wait seemed interminable, but I couldn't get mad at the good woman, who would offer me a crispy coconut cookie and coddle me with hands that smelled of sweet detergent when she found me.

I tried to memorize a few sections of the library. I learned, for example, that after the section "Birds of Paradise," one could find "Planes and Parachutists," and after the section "Whirlpools in the Sea and in Hair" came "Wigs of Famous Heads."

Some names made me laugh; others worried me. One day I passed through the section "People Who Cough Too Much." There I found a book titled *Smokers Who Suffer*. Immediately I thought of my mother. What would she be doing? Had she worn again the mustard-colored sweater, with its turtleneck, that made her look so pretty?

That night I took another spoonful of iron. I couldn't disappoint my mother. That dark substance tasted as bad as ever. Luckily, I had the anise drops Catalina had given me. I thought of her thin hands, which when they were at rest seemed to say something, something good and calm. Looking at them was enough to know that everything could be better.

The next day I forgot to take my iron, but not the anise drop.

My uncle had told me that the books moved, but it couldn't be true. I memorized various titles, remembering where they were, and for various days I saw them in the same place.

However, as soon as I began to look for a book that Catalina might like, something strange happened. The section "Birds of Paradise" remained in its place, but I couldn't find the book titled *The Dalmatian Rooster*, which normally began that section. The same thing happened to me when I reached "Planes and Skydivers." I spent hours searching for *Bubble Gum Bombers*, which I had always been able to find before.

What was happening? Uncle had said that the books moved during my earlier visits. This time, it had only started happening after having gone to the pharmacy. Had Catalina affected me so much that I had started affecting the books?

Had I contracted something from her, or had some dormant force in me now been awoken?

Everything was very strange, and very interesting.

I wandered the hallways in search of a book she might like. I couldn't fail her. I had to find something really special.

I went to the section "Magnificent Dogs." I had always loved dogs. Pinta was a small Maltese and I dreamed of having a Labrador that would leap onto my bed at night.

I looked through every kind of canine adventure until I found a book that was there by mistake, for it didn't have anything to do with the subject: *Journey Along the Heart-Shaped River*. I opened it out of simple curiosity, but it hooked me right away.

I couldn't take my eyes off that story. It was about two boys, Ernesto and Pepe, who got lost in the forest, built canoes from a tree trunk, and decided to each search for a different way out of there. One went toward the East, and the other toward the West, but the river was shaped like a heart and, after a thousand incidents and adventures, they were reunited at the same spot, where an Indian helped them to build an enormous bonfire made from dry branches. The Indian explained to them that the forest was so thick that not even the eagles, with their magnificent vision, could know if someone were there. That place on the river was the only spot that was clear enough to send a smoke signal up into the sky. "Here is where the heart beats," the Indian explained. Then he told them his name: Eagle Eye. The flames of the bonfire rose up into the skies and were seen by the eagles, who flew in circles around them, and then by a helicopter that had come to rescue the lost children. Before the hydrohelicopter landed on the river, the Indian showed Pepe and Ernesto how to make a compass with twigs and a stone; then he disappeared into the underbrush.

That same afternoon I took the book to Catalina. She wasn't there, so I didn't get nervous. I left it with her mother, a very quiet and friendly woman.

I also took advantage of being there to talk to my mother on the phone. She sounded much calmer. Her voice sounded firm, as if she took iron every morning. Curiously, this worried me: she seemed to need me less than before.

She told me that she had dyed her hair and that seemed strange to me.

"Are you blonde now?" I asked.

"Can you imagine?" she exclaimed, and laughed.

"What then?"

"I dyed my hair my same color."

This seemed even stranger to me. Why would someone dye their hair the same color they already had?

"It's because of the gray hairs," she explained. "I feel better now."

However, as she said this I heard an unmistakable sound: she had lit a match. She paused to take a drag. Mama still needed me. I knew by the way she puffed and coughed from the smoke.

"And how are you?" she asked after clearing her throat. "Fine," I lied.

When I hung up the phone, it seemed to me that the receiver smelled like ash. After my midafternoon snack, my uncle wanted to play a board game where Romans fought against Carthaginians. The Romans went on foot and the Carthaginians rode on elephants. I preferred to look for another book. I returned to the section "Magnificent Dogs" and once again stumbled upon an unexpected volume: *Fire on the Heart-Shaped River*. The same characters returned to the forest. This time, some tourists tried to make Eagle Eye's bonfire, but they did it in the wrong place, creating a terrible forest fire. The deer, the foxes, and the bears ran to save themselves and took refuge in a place where the river wasn't very deep and they could still poke their noses out to breathe. Ernesto and Pepe had to make a long detour to reach the place where the heart of the forest beat, and they were forced to swim the last segment. When they finally reached the right place, they discovered that their matches had gotten wet. Taking advantage of the sunlight, they used their eyeglasses as magnifying glasses to burn the dry leaves. That's how they built up a good-sized bonfire. This time they acted without the Indian's help, for he was trapped on the other side of the fire. The hydrohelicopter reached the river and showed off another of its resources: it had a canister that could suck up water and throw it on the fire. The children helped to put out the flames, then they went up into the helicopter and saw Eagle Eye in the distance; he had saved himself by swimming on a tree trunk to the other side of the river.

The next day I found other stories of the Heart-Shaped River, in sections of the library that had nothing to do with them.

I mentioned this to my uncle, who thought it was the most natural thing in the world.

"I told you already that the books move around. Something has changed in you. When I met you, I knew that you were a boy who attracted stories. Not anyone makes the books reorganize themselves and try to reach them. You have that power, but you must learn how to use it. When your mother brought you, you acted like you were dazed. I thought you had lost your powers. You returned to the library looking a bit lost. I guessed that you'd had some problems." Tito looked at me very seriously, as he had never done before. "I understand you, Nephew, I also know what it is like to feel very alone. Sometimes I like it, but sometimes I feel weary of it. I think that you are recovering your strength. Something important has happened."

I didn't want to talk about who I had been talking to in the pharmacy.

"The books feel their readers," my uncle continued. "Not just anyone deserves to read them. Something has opened within you. The effect is contagious, even I have seen books that I don't remember having bought. Do you know what I've just read?"

"What?" I asked, fearful that Uncle would make another of his pauses to go to the bathroom.

Luckily, this time my curiosity was satisfied right away.

My uncle opened the book with the blue cover that had arrived a few days before.

"It says here that when the energy of a reader is too strong, it could produce a book storm. That is the Lector Princeps Tempestus. The shelves move in a whirlwind like a real cyclone. This has happened a few times: one Greek in the Library of Alexandria, a short-tempered Italian monk in the Middle Ages, and an Argentine in the library on Calle Mexico in Buenos Aires. These are all very isolated cases. Normally books move without your being able to see that they move. Their leaps are invisible. Suddenly they're in front of you."

"Who were those Lectors Tempestus?" I asked, very intrigued.

"Eratosthenes, the librarian of Alexandria, who calculated the circumference of the Earth. The Library of Alexandria was one of the Seven Wonders of the World. As for the medieval monk, he was a man who prayed with his eyes closed, giving his books the chance to act in secret. The Argentine was blind and couldn't see how those volumes he knew by memory moved about. Sometimes, the greatest readers are those who have an impediment. This library was created by my father, who was also blind."

Uncle stared at me with his enormous eyes, as if I were much farther away and he were trying to make out my features.

"Why are you looking at me like that?" I asked.

"I always look at you like this."

"Sometimes it frightens me that you stare at me so much."

"Sorry, Nephew. It's a bad habit. It comes from having lived with someone who was blind. I used to stare at my father all the time. I did so blatantly because he couldn't see me. I was very interested in observing his reactions. For example, he always knew if it were night or day, although he couldn't see. He turned his head as if he were seeking the light from a window. Sometimes he could feel the heat of the sun and perhaps a glimmer reached the depths of his eyes, but sometimes he knew what time it was without having any way of orienting himself. The blind have a very precise inner vision, they develop a powerful memory, they hear sounds that turn into images for them. They transform the world into a clock of sounds. I read to my father and from his gestures I could tell that he saw the powerful images the books spoke of. I got used to tracking all of his gestures. He didn't see, and I saw him too much. That's why my eyes are sometimes too big when I'm with other people. I'm not discreet at all. I beg your pardon."

This long and sincere explanation surprised me very much.

"Don't worry, Uncle," I told him.

"Sometimes I miss him," he commented in a low voice. "My father got me hooked on reading and showed me that a book is better when shared. How good it is that now I have you!" He smiled with teeth as long as a horse's.

At that moment, Eufrosia arrived with hot chocolate and little pastries. Uncle popped an entire pastry in his mouth and kept talking. His pants became covered by pink-colored crumbs. I made a gesture to him to be quiet and to eat in peace.

Tito was so impatient that he was used to boiling temperatures; he couldn't wait for drinks to grow cold. He took a sip of chocolate and I thought I could see the smoke come out of his ears. Then he said, "The books feel confident before a magnificent reader who has bad vision or closes their eyes. Then they move even more, to the point of provoking severe storms. There are tales of people who have died buried beneath various encyclopedias. I tell you this so you might be careful. The most difficult aspect of having a power is learning not to use it or to use it only when it is necessary. You attract books. That is a very important ability, but you must control that gift."

I didn't feel special at all. The only thing I wanted was to keep finding stories about the Heart-Shaped River to give to Catalina.

The Story a Book Tells
Is Not Always
the Same

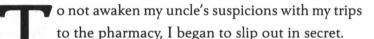

To not awaken my uncle's suspicions with my trips to the pharmacy, I began to slip out in secret.

I waited for the moment when he went into the fern room or some distant part of the library, and I took the keys that Eufrosia hung from a nail in the kitchen.

Catalina liked *Journey Along the Heart-Shaped River* so much that she wouldn't put it down, not even when she had to wrap the leg of a lady who had twisted her ankle. She finished the last chapter in between giving two injections.

Her reading had been more agitated and perhaps more emotional than my own. It had also been somewhat different. She surprised me tremendously when she said, "I liked the girl a lot."

I was about to ask, "What girl?" but Catalina couldn't say anything without my being in agreement with her.

"And Ernesto?" I asked her.

"Him too, although he's a bit conceited."

"And Pepe?"

"What Pepe?" was her surprising reply.

I had read the story of two boys, Ernesto and Pepe. She, on the other hand, had read the story of Ernesto and Marina. Perhaps she was so distracted selling pills and wrapping wounds that she had imagined another story.

She returned the book to me and I gave her the next.

"You've got something on you there," she told me, when I said goodbye.

Catalina stuck her hand through my hair and pulled out a long red thread.

"It looks like a hair from a doll." Catalina smiled and I could see her magnificent twisted tooth.

My uncle's curtains were red, his pajamas were red, and his robe was red. The thread must have come from one of those fabrics.

"Here, let me fix your hair," she told me.

She ran her hands over me. It was as if her fingers placed a crown on my head. I gave her the book and returned home to reread *Journey Along the Heart-Shaped River*.

I poured myself a glass of milk, but the book soon captured my attention so thoroughly that I left the glass untouched. The book had changed! It was no longer the story of Ernesto and Pepe, but of Ernesto and Marina. It seemed to me that Ernesto was, indeed, a bit conceited.

Was it possible that I hadn't read the book properly before?

That night I wanted to talk with my uncle about the strange change in the story in the forest, but he didn't come down to dinner.

"He left the house," Eufrosia told me. "We ran out of tea, and he can't live without his fifteen cups a day."

I woke very early, anxious to talk with my uncle. He was taking so long in coming down to the kitchen that I decided to go look for him in his bedroom.

It was the first time I'd been there. His room was in the highest part of the house. The last steps to reach his door were books.

When I entered, he was still fast asleep. He had a book over his face, the pages fluttering with each of his snores.

My father always got angry when I had a nightmare and woke him up at night. My uncle, on the other hand, seemed to think it perfectly normal for me to be there, eager to talk to him.

"It's good to have a morning conversation," he said enthusiastically, "but I am like a blank book this early. I need tea for the words to reach me."

I went down to the kitchen and Eufrosia gave me a thermos. With that much tea we could talk for a few hours. I went back up to his bedroom. My uncle was still lying in bed, but he looked at me with alert eyes.

"Push back the curtains so that the room might shine with the intensity of Borges's prose," he requested.

I slid the red curtains back and the sun flooded the chamber.

"There is no better prose than light," Uncle said.

He spoke in a strange way, as if he were still asleep.

"What is prose?" I asked him.

"The art of putting words together that don't make verse. It is the way in which you and I speak. We communicate in prose, although sometimes we make a verse without meaning to. What did you want to ask me?"

"Is it possible for a book to change when it is read by another person?" I asked him.

I told him what had happened with Catalina, without mentioning her by name.

"What you tell me is interesting, very interesting," Uncle said. He opened the thermos and the air filled with the smell of smoke. "Every book is like a mirror: it reflects what you think. It is not the same if it is read by a hero than if it is read by a villain. The great readers add something to books, they make them better. But very rarely does something like what you told me take place. When someone modifies a book for you and you can tell, it means that you've reached a way of reading that resembles a river. No river remains still, Nephew, its waters change."

"Has it ever happened to you?"

My uncle looked away, something he had never done before. He looked restlessly toward a corner of the room and then said in a strange voice, "A long time ago. I was very young, my dear Nephew, and so was she. But I was frightened by how the stories changed before my eyes."

"Did they become tales of terror?"

"No, they became more interesting, but what frightened me was that she had such power. It seemed too strong to me, uncontrollable, and I stopped seeing her. Many years later she worked as a professor at a famous university. She sent me a postcard and I regretted having been afraid of her powers as a reader. It is what I most regret in my life. Then I got married, but she didn't love books and I had to leave her. That's why I remain here in this library alone. Well, until you got here." It was the second time he said that in a very short span of time.

My uncle's story made me feel sad. It seemed to make him sad as well, because he proposed, "Let's go to the kitchen for some coconut cookies. We need something to sweeten this day that has already turned sour."

Four days later, I went to retrieve the second book that I had loaned Catalina. I breathed in the smell of the pharmacy that I so liked. She was busy with some clients. I saw the telephone and decided to call my mother.

"King Juancholoncito," she said. I was terribly embarrassed whenever she called me Juancholoncito.

I turned bright red. At that moment, Catalina looked up at me and I wanted to become invisible. She waved at me from far away, showing that she had the book ready to give back to me.

My mother sounded content, so much so that she called me once more by that ridiculous nickname.

Then something curious happened. Whenever I thought of Mama I usually wanted to be with her. I imagined helping her and making her happy. Now, for the first time, I spoke to her calmly and didn't even wonder if she was smoking, as if her problems weren't mine. I hung up and approached Catalina.

I heard her listing off the strange names of some vaccines. Then she turned toward me, happy to see me.

"This one is even better." She pointed to the book.

Without replying I returned to my uncle's house, eager to reread it.

Catalina had added wonderful details to the adventure. Ernesto and Marina managed to flee along a path that burned above them like a tunnel of flame.

At first, Ernesto didn't dare to run through the tunnel, but she took his hand and her bravery gave him courage.

Marina had a pleasant and firm nature. Ernesto, who seemed a bit conceited before, now acted with simplicity and helped Marina climb out of a hole she'd fallen into; he took off his shirt, dipped it in the river and gave it to her to wipe the mud off.

In the end, when they had been saved, they swam in the cold water. Marina played at being a fish and bit Ernesto.

That night I dreamed I was in a river.

The Shadow Books

Until this moment, I haven't dared to write about something that happened during those days, which affected me very strongly. Although much time has passed since then, I shall try to recount the incidents of that wondrous summer as if they were happening in front of me.

I went to the section "Magnificent Dogs" in search of more stories about the Heart-Shaped River. However, I couldn't find any. Some books caught my interest with their titles about adventures and their splendid full-color illustrations, but I wasn't interested in anything other than returning to the forest where Ernesto and Marina lived their adventures.

Did other stories on the river exist? What could I do to find them? Would they arrive on their own so I could read them?

Life in Uncle Tito's house had turned out to be more interesting than I had foreseen. Sometimes, though, he seemed to me to be a bit sad, as if he regretted having spent so many years without any company other than his cats and his books. I was also unsettled when he stared at me with his bug-eyed look, as if he were expecting something of me. I liked being a Lector Princeps, because I had never been praised in that way before, but I was afraid of disappointing my uncle. Perhaps my reading powers weren't as intense as he believed.

In my first weeks in the library I more or less stuck to the same areas. There were so many books and so many rooms that I got lost easily and often had to ring the bell to be rescued by my uncle.

My uncle's library was so big I hadn't been able to explore all of it, but I still didn't dare go too far into its depths. What might happen if I went to a place so distant that my bell couldn't be heard? Nonetheless, I couldn't stop wondering what there might be in the remotest corners of the house. Books about horrors and black magic? Texts about crimes, written in blood?

Since my favorite country was Australia, I also thought that perhaps there was some pleasant, faraway place in the library, an Australia of books, which very few people had managed to reach. Would there be strange and fascinating books there, like the koala, the kangaroo, and the platypus?

One afternoon, I dared to go a bit farther than usual. I went down a long hallway, carpeted in a wine-colored rug. I kept walking until I noticed a strange smell. More than a scent, what I perceived was the sensation that this place had been closed up, as if nobody had breathed in there for a long time, as if everything had been still, very still, and my nose suddenly shook it all up. It smelled of old books that didn't seem to be preserved there, but instead seemed to be the room's prisoners. I picked up the book closest to me and a cloud of dust powdered my face. It was thick dust, like breadcrumbs. I took a few more steps and the sensation of being enclosed became stronger. I didn't dare keep breathing that dense, dead air.

I returned feeling rather befuddled and didn't want to have dinner. The dust had spoiled my appetite.

That night the scarlet dream returned. Once more I walked down a damp and dark hallway to the room where a woman cried. Once more my hands were stained with blood when I touched the walls.

I woke up early in the morning, drenched in sweat. I was very thirsty, but I was afraid to go down to the kitchen in those dark hours. I remained in bed, trying to calm myself.

I thought of the hallway where I had been that afternoon and of its wine-colored carpeting. Compared to my nightmare, that place wasn't so terrible. It was a closed-up space, full of old books, but nothing more.

I didn't like how it smelled in there and I'd felt uncomfortable, but it was something that could be endured. On the other hand, I was unbearably afraid of closed doors. Perhaps there was nothing behind them, but I imagined horrible things, like the blood that flooded the scarlet room.

It occurred to me that if I dared to explore the entire library I would no longer be afraid of the unknown corners of the house, and perhaps I might also stop having the scarlet dream.

If I plucked up the courage to visit every room, there would no longer be any reason for me to fear any of them, not even the one that appeared in my dreams.

The next day, I mentioned to my uncle that some places in the house smelled all locked-up, like a prison.

"You're right, Nephew. Ventilation is not the house's specialty. There are little vents in the roof so that air can come in. Normally they're closed, to keep pollution, or sometimes an adventurous bird, from coming in. But you can open them if you suffer a lack of oxygen."

"How?"

"In this city the wind blows from north to south. On the walls that face north, you'll find cords that open the vents."

"How will I know which walls face north?"

"If you don't know anything about geography, don't worry. Just pull whenever you see a rope."

I went to the hallway with the wine-colored rug. Between two bookshelves, I managed to make out a very worn cord. I pulled on it and it snapped in my fingers. That's how old it was.

Further in I found another rope and I pulled on it. After a few seconds, I felt a slight breeze. The atmosphere changed completely, touched by an invisible freshness, and I felt calmer. Things started to seem not locked in but guarded, protected.

I continued forward but didn't venture too far, for I still wasn't completely confident. I opened vents every time it was necessary, scanning sections and shelves, but I didn't find any more adventures of the Heart-Shaped River.

I began to explore the library more confidently, but the fruitlessness of my search soon soured my mood. I scanned the shelves in different ways. First with curiosity, then with urgency, and finally with desperation.

My feet hurt and I was starving when I discovered that I was lost. What I feared most had happened. My bravery had turned to carelessness. Uncle Tito had warned me to manage my strength, but I had followed his advice too late.

I rang the bell for a long time, but I did so in vain.

I was in a room with an arched ceiling. High above me I thought I saw a dove painted, or perhaps it was just a whitish stain. The room had four doors and I didn't recognize any of them.

I had already gotten lost on other occasions without it being a problem, since I had not gone very far from the living room and the kitchen.

"Uncle Tito!" I shouted.

The books absorbed my words. There were so many of them and they were so thick that they ate up any sound.

"Eufrosia!" That shout wasn't heard either.

It was no use wasting my strength shouting. What would Ernesto and Marina have done in a similar situation? They oriented themselves easily in the forest, and in a certain way the library was a forest since the pages of the books came from trees. How would my heroes have gotten out of a written forest?

If I were the character of a story and I was on page 78, what would I do to reach the next chapter?

Thinking of Ernesto and Marina gave me courage. Since there were four doors, I thought they must represent the directions of a map: north, south, east, and west.

I went to the door that I took to represent the west. I peeked into a large room. Astonishingly, it contained no books, but instead taxidermy animal heads. One of my uncles had been a famous hunter.

There were deer, rams, boars, coyotes, wolves, and a bear. I would have preferred to see those animals in the forest of the stories (except for the bear and the wolves, who had enormous fangs). In any event, I admired the beauty of those savage animals. Some of the deer had enormous antlers. Uncle Tito had told me that the importance of a deer was determined by the number of points its antlers had. I counted all of them and saw that there was one with fourteen points. Who would have dared to kill that king of the deer? I was ashamed that someone of my own family might have once done so. The deer had black glass eyes. Its gray pelt darkened under its eyes, following a track that looked like a tear or perhaps a question mark. This gave the animal a sad aspect, as if it had cried. I didn't think that the exit could be through this room and decided to try another.

This time I went to the door that I took to represent the east. Once again, I entered a room that held no books. An empty room. I approached one of the walls. It was covered in damp spots. Saltpeter covered its surface in enormous bubbles. Books would have been destroyed in this place. Why hadn't they called a plumber? Uncle Tito's house was stranger than I had imagined.

This room was populated with statues of people reading. From their clothes, I understood that they were ancient people. At the base of each statue I found inscriptions in unknown languages.

For a moment, I wondered if they were men who had become petrified in the library. Perhaps it was a strange museum of readers.

The dust made me sneeze and I decided to leave.

I peeked through the south door but I didn't dare enter that room, which was full of diminutive books, as if the library had shrunk. I was disconcerted to see so many tiny books, printed with text the size of an ant's eye. What a terrible effort it would be to read all those volumes! If there was a copy of one of the stories of the Heart-Shaped River there, it would have stood out like a giant among elves. I had to look elsewhere.

I decided to try the north door, the last one left. This time I didn't know what lay on the other side because everything was dark. I had never experienced a greater darkness. My eyes filled with blackness. I held a finger before my eyelashes and I couldn't see it.

I took one step, and a second, and then started to fear I'd get lost. I turned around—I had made the mistake of closing the door and now I couldn't see it! I tried to walk toward it. I touched the wall, feeling all along it, but my hands didn't detect any trace of the door nor the jamb. That wall was despairingly smooth.

What was I to do? My heart pounded in my chest. I stood in silence for a moment, listening to my agitated breathing.

Suddenly, a pleasant smell reached me, as if there were a slight breeze. If the air was moving, that meant that there must be a window somewhere.

What did that current of air smell like? Like the sheets at home. A clean smell that made you feel happy.

I moved in that direction, but then paid dearly for my daring. I banged heavily into something solid. I touched it carefully: it was a bookshelf. I caressed the spine of a book, a smooth spine, made of leather. Although I couldn't see anything, I opened it and ran my hands over its pages; I felt the raised bumps of writing for the blind. I touched dots and small dashes. These must've belonged to my great-uncle, Tito's father, who was blind. That's why the room was so dark.

The darkness wasn't due to anything malign. For my great-uncle, this was surely a quiet and pleasant place, where he could read books that transported him to brilliant worlds full of color.

This idea calmed me and let me keep moving between the bookcases.

From time to time I stopped to touch some pages, just for the pleasure of doing so. My fingers slid over the letters for the blind. I tried to imagine what those little points and lines meant for someone who knew how to read by touch: battles, desert crossings, dragons with mouths of flame, ships about to founder.

I was doing just this when I heard a sound. A book fell from somewhere. Immediately afterwards, I heard other books falling to the floor. Was there someone here?

I shouted as loudly as I could. The books swallowed my words and the room returned to silence. Not the slightest whisper could be heard.

I was overcome by a terrible fright, as if the wall from my nightmares lay at the end of the room. Had I finally fallen into my own dream? I had wanted to run through all the rooms in the house to leave behind my fear of that scarlet room, but now I felt trapped in my nightmare. Why had I ever believed myself brave enough to come this far? And if I suddenly heard a woman's cries? I covered my ears.

Then I sat down on the floor, unable to move. I spent a long time like that.

Suddenly, I felt something at the nape of my neck. A page from a book. Worse yet, it wasn't a still page! It was a page that had moved. I could feel its caress.

I thought someone was going to kill me, and I thought of all the things I'd never be able to do again. And I thought of my sister, Carmen, and my mother's smile; of my father; of my curious and beloved uncle; of Pablo, my great friend; and then, with a strong trembling, I thought of Catalina and her honey-colored eyes, which made me feel like a better person every time she looked at me. Seated there in the darkness, surrounded by an unknown danger, I knew that I had too many things to lose if I didn't get out of that room.

I stood up, a bit stiff from having sat so long. I thought I could make out a gust of fresh air to my right. I moved in that direction.

Another book fell right beside me, then a second. Who was throwing them? What on earth was going on?

I thought I was going crazy. Then I remembered something that Uncle Tito said: when the books know they're not seen, they might cause a storm. This time they didn't slide discreetly toward me, without my seeing them advance; they leaped and jumped from everywhere.

The books moved haphazardly. They acted at whim, but not necessarily against me. Perhaps they were just having fun. I calmed down a little and managed to weave my way through them.

I had to hurry to reach the exit before the books could block it.

I walked as fast as I could, leaping over books, stepping on some, and little by little I understood what was happening. The books were forming into a stairway beneath my feet. They didn't want to hinder my leaving, they were trying to help.

I climbed up and up, using the books as steps. I kept thinking that my head would soon bang against the ceiling, but the room was very high, perhaps the highest in the entire house.

I was exhausted from climbing the books, which kept creating new steps. Then I felt something delightful: fresh wind on my face. There had to be a window nearby.

My outstretched hands managed to touch the wall. I carefully felt along the surface until I made out a hollow space. I peeked into it: it led to a narrow tunnel. At the end of it I saw a small, blue circle: the sky.

I climbed into the tunnel, which was barely wider than my body, and crawled forward.

After a few minutes, I reached the end. I looked down and could see the garden. I had never been so high up in a house. I reached out and my hands touched something metallic. It was a ladder, like those in a ship. I could climb down it.

I went down into the garden. I was astonished by my adventure, my head was a tumult of ideas, but before I could sort out my thoughts I heard my uncle's voice.

"I've been waiting for you for five cups of tea, now," he said, smiling. "I see you discovered the room of the Shadow Books. My father liked to lock himself in there. He liked to be alone, in the dark, without anyone to bother him. Sometimes I joined him there, with a book and a flashlight. This book you've brought with you must come from those days."

"What book I've brought with me?" I asked, very surprised.

"The one sticking out of the pocket of your jacket."

I patted all my pockets. With enormous surprise, I realized that a book had slipped into one of them.

But what amazed me even more was its title: *A Discovery on the Heart-Shaped River.*

The Wild Book

I had never seen my uncle in the garden. He walked on the grass in a funny way, as if he were afraid of squishing it.

I wasn't surprised when he said, "Enough fresh air. Let's go back to the house."

He headed toward the door that led to the greenhouse, where Eufrosia had left us a thermos of tea, a glass of chocolate milk, and boar's ham sandwiches.

I asked my uncle what had happened.

"You need to recover your strength after your big adventure," he answered. "You're making great progress. You've already discovered the room with the taxidermy animals and the room with the statues. You've reached them much sooner than I imagined. Did you see the photographs?"

"What photographs?"

"Of the family. They're hanging on the wall, in the room with the statues. They're in one corner."

"I didn't see them."

"I'm not surprised. The statues have much more presence. In any case, I recommend you pay more attention. Sometimes the biggest secrets lie in the smallest details."

"And who hunted those animals?"

"Our ancestors were great hunters. They were rather primitive people who thought that killing could be a sport. I prefer adventures where nobody sheds any blood."

"In the stories of the river, sometimes there is an accident and someone gets cut and they bleed," I commented.

"And it's right that things should be that way; those adventures take place in a forest full of dangers. The blood that bothers me is the stuff that drips in real life. Luckily, there are people like your friend in the pharmacy who can bandage one up again."

I was surprised. I thought my visits to Catalina were a secret.

"Who told you that I have a friend in the pharmacy?" I asked.

"This house's fount of knowledge: Eufrosia."

"What a gossip!"

"She is only looking out for you. She told me that the girl in question is named Catalina, that she is pretty, and that she loves books. It seems that you've loaned her some from this library."

I thought that Uncle Tito was going to reproach me for having done so, but he added good-naturedly, "You shouldn't feel bad. Books exist to be shared. Moreover, it's always good to have someone handy who can ease your pains with creams and pills. Speaking of which, how long has it been since you last took your iron? Your mother asked me to make sure you take it."

"I no longer need it," I answered. "I haven't had any cramps."

I thought he was going to force me to drink those disgusting spoonfuls of black syrup that tasted like nails. But instead he said, "You're maturing, my nephew. Besides, I don't like to take syrups for things I can find naturally in my food. Whoever needs iron should chew on some spinach or eat a nice liver steak. Or if they're truly desperate, lick a knife. Sometimes science exaggerates and wants to give us pills and syrups for everything. Soon they'll be inventing a syrup for books that concentrates all stories into a single spoonful!"

Once more, Tito was wandering on a tangent. It was difficult for him to follow the thread of a conversation.

I took a delicious sip of chocolate milk and asked him, "Why do you have statues in the house?"

"For the same reason I keep those stuffed animals: they're lovely and I haven't dared to throw them out. My great-great-grandfather ordered them made in the Greek style. They are statues of great readers. Before, there was a statue in every room of the house, as a sort of guardian. But they were very scary. Just imagine if you wake up at night, needing to use the bathroom, you get out of bed and suddenly see an enormous man made from marble. Not everyone recovers from such a shock. That's why I sent them all to the Room of Readers. If someone is interested in the faces of the first people who read for pleasure, they can go and visit them. I also recommend you take a look at the photographs of the family. There you'll find people you know, and, by the way, how did you get on with the Shadow Books?"

"They moved."

"They moved! Why didn't you tell me before? And we're sitting here nattering on about sucking on knives!"

My uncle brought his face up close to mine. He hadn't shaved in a few days and his bristles looked like porcupine spines. He smelled of worn sheets. It was a relief when he pulled back and asked more calmly, "Did they move a little or a lot?"

"A lot."

"Did they slither like vipers in the grass without your seeing them, or did they storm about the room?"

"In neither of those two ways."

"Can you describe what happened?" He gave me a sandwich and said, "Boar's ham clears the mind. Chew and then swallow a bite. I am all aquiver to hear your response."

I liked the sandwich more than ever. It was lighter and tastier than the best salami.

"Go on," my uncle said.

"First I thought that the books were falling."

"Falling like rain or falling like a waterfall?"

"One by one."

"Rockfall!" Uncle declared.

"Then I thought they were going to squash me."

"Squash you like one squashes an ant or like you've been hit with a pillow?" Uncle was endlessly curious about every last detail.

"Squash as if everything were trembling and were threatening to come crashing down."

"Trembling books! That hasn't happened in a long time. They need a special shaking to act that way. And then what happened?"

"I walked and stumbled until the books began to fall into order."

"Do you mean to say, my dear nephew, that the books came to an agreement among themselves as to how they should move?"

"Yes."

My uncle's eyes looked like they would leap right off of his face.

"Are you sure?" he asked. His mouth was open so wide in shock, it looked as if he wanted to swallow up what I was about to say in a single gulp.

"Yes," I answered. And he snapped his lips shut as if he were swallowing a pill.

"I want you to remember that I am your Uncle Ernesto, known as Tito, and that I've promised your mother to feed you and take care of you. It is important that you tell me the truth because this could have very significant consequences."

"I am telling the truth."

"I believe you, Nephew, I haven't doubted you. It's just that . . . there are things that are difficult to verify." He sipped his tea so nervously that he spilled it on his pants.

He was so interested in my story that he didn't even mind having stained himself. He looked at me with utter focus, as if I were a difficult-to-locate fish at the bottom of an aquarium, and asked in a low but intense voice, "Do you know what I think?"

"No."

"The books have already read you."

"What?"

"There are people who think they understand a book just because they know how to read. I already told you that books are like mirrors: every person finds in them what they have in their own head. The problem is that you only discover what you have inside you when you read the right book. Books are indiscreet and risky mirrors: they make your most original ideas take flight, inspiring thoughts you never knew you had. When you don't read, those thoughts remain prisoners in your head. They're no use at all."

"I also learn things from books that would have never occurred to me," I said.

"Of course. A magic mirror is still a window: in it you see your own ideas, meet the ideas of others, and visit different worlds. A book is the best means of transportation: it carries you far, doesn't pollute, arrives on time, is inexpensive, and never gives you motion sickness."

"But what's so special about me to the books? I'm not even a good student."

"My dear Juan, it's not necessary to be very diligent to become a great reader. My books feel that you could love them like nobody has loved them and that you can share them with someone whom you love dearly, like the girl in the pharmacy, who has such lovely eyes."

"Eufrosia told you she has lovely eyes?"

"It's not always necessary to rely on what the newscasters tell you. I had an urge for more aspirins, so I went to the pharmacy myself. Catalina has lovely eyes. But she also has deep eyes. She improved the story you read, *River*, isn't that so?"

"Yes."

"An ideal reader! Now tell me something and don't make a mistake because this is important. You said the books moved in order. Could you tell me exactly what they did?"

"They formed steps."

"Steps!" Uncle shouted the word with obvious admiration.

"Yes."

"Like a staircase?"

"Is there another way for steps to be?"

"Of course not. My excitement is making me silly. How many steps were there?"

"I didn't count them. I climbed up them until I'd reached the ceiling of the room."

"You reached the ceiling?"

"That's how I got out through the window."

"Of course, of course . . ." Uncle began to walk in circles. He passed right beside a fern from the greenhouse. Without realizing it, he plucked a leaf from it. He held it as if it were a sword and crossed it over his breast. "Something has happened that has never before been seen in this library. You are very special."

"I feel the same as always."

"That just means that you're super-extra-special. People who give themselves airs of importance aren't special, they're just vain. Geniuses are simple: they don't think they're geniuses."

"I'm not a genius, Uncle, I'm your nephew."

"I don't want to make your head swim with so many eulogies. You're good and simple and you like salami, just like those great readers who are now statues, although I don't know if they ate salami."

"I don't want to be a statue, Uncle."

"Nor do you need to be. You're going to be something much better."

"What's that?"

"The tamer of *The Wild Book*."

Uncle froze with his jaws wide open, impressed by his own words. One could have stuck an entire sandwich into his mouth. But I was more curious than I was in the mood for playing tricks, so I merely asked, "Can you explain this to me a little more?"

"I need to do a lot of explaining."

"The book you're looking for is called *The Wild Book*?"

"That is its title, Nephew. I haven't told anyone before."

"Well, tell me more."

"Before I say anything, I must tell you that it is very rare for the books to move in synchrony and even rarer for them to form steps. That means that they place themselves at your feet and are ready to take you wherever you need to go. You'll always find a book that helps you. Books are loyal. No soldier has ever fought as hard for his country as a book does for its reader."

"And are there no bad books?"

"It's curious that you should ask me that. Yes, my nephew, there are bad books, very bad ones. I don't refer to badly made or ridiculous books, the sad books written by a person who suffered without that suffering being useful, the books made by idiots who only wanted to be famous. No, I refer to books that do damage and attack other books. It's not easy to recognize them, because they're clever and hide their true message. If you read them, they can seem pleasant, but they make you forget what other books say. Great readers don't let themselves be fooled, but sometimes even they accept that venom, made of oblivion and bad intention. I must confess something to you."

A chunk of sandwich sank unchewed into my stomach. Uncle continued, "This library is not free of malign books. One must be alert. Sometimes they arrive disguised as useful books, like dictionaries or cookbooks. But that's not the most important thing that I wanted to tell you."

Uncle stretched out the fern leaf and exclaimed, "This summer will be decisive for you!"

I thought, "It's already so complicated that it hardly feels like a break," but I didn't dare say so out loud.

At that moment, Eufrosia entered the greenhouse. "How hot it is in here! Are you going to want to have chicken for dinner or should I make pizza?"

"How can you interrupt us for that?" Uncle asked, very upset. "We are about to say something that could change the history of mankind and you show up talking about pizza. A pizza is a circle of hot flour splattered with sauce. Could a circle of hot flour splattered with sauce matter to us?"

"I want pizza," I said.

Uncle abruptly changed his mind. "Perfect, Nephew, whatever you want." He turned to look at Eufrosia. "Are you still here? We need a pizza right away!"

The good woman left the room muttering.

"What is *The Wild Book* like?" I dared to ask.

"I don't know. I told you it has never been read."

"Nobody has ever found it?"

"It is lost in the library. My great-great-grandfather had it in his hands, also my great-grandfather, my grandfather, and my father. None of them could read it. It escaped from all of them. It is a rebellious book, which will only allow itself to be read when someone can manage to tame it, like a wild horse tamed by a rider."

"And it remains here in the library?"

"It has changed its location, but it can't have left."

"How do you know?"

"Because it is looking for you."

At that moment, I felt a whirlwind under my feet. I was suddenly so exhausted from everything that had happened to me with the Shadow Books. I felt my eyelids droop, and when I regained consciousness, I was on the kitchen table. Uncle and Eufrosia had carried me there. The cook placed a damp cloth on my forehead and made me smell some spicy salts.

"What happened?" I asked, seeing the cook's hands, reddish from washing so many dishes and from coming so close to the cooking flames.

"Do you recognize me?" Uncle asked.

"Of course I do."

"We'll see. What am I called: Tati, Tito, or Toti?"

How was it possible for someone to be both so intelligent and so childish?

To mess with him, I said, "You're my Aunt Tati."

"It can't be!" he howled. "My beloved nephew has lost his mind! We were about to resolve the enigma of *The Wild Book*. What terrible luck! Now what shall I tell his mother?

All we need now is for you to suddenly sprout feathers or to want to become a singing sensation on some TV show where you dance like a robot! Did you turn into a singing dummy?"

I felt so sorry to see him like this that I immediately retracted myself.

"It was just a joke, Uncle Tito."

Then he kissed my cheeks and rubbed my head in a very strange way, as if he were drying a plate with a tea towel. It seemed he didn't have much experience expressing affection. This made me think of my mother, who hugged me as if she were a specialist in making people feel better. Poor Uncle had never had anyone who comforted him like that. For him, showing affection to another person was as complicated as opening a locked safe.

It didn't surprise me that he should say, "I've been alone for too long, Nephew. That's why I asked your mother for you to come here. I believed in your powers, but I didn't know they were so strong. The books have been moving since you got here and you've just overcome the test of darkness: they took advantage of the darkness to coordinate their movements, and they even made a staircase for you. You are their master. They will help you find *The Wild Book*. If you manage to tame it, you can read the story you've always wanted."

"Who wrote this book?"

"I don't know. The books are more important than their authors. The best books seem to write themselves. *The Wild*

Book needs a special reader, and I think it's you. Welcome to the library, brave Nephew!"

Uncle spoke to me as if I had just that moment arrived at the house, and in a certain way that was true: from that moment on, my life would be different.

The Wild Book had not allowed anyone to approach it. Would it let me be the one to read it?

The Story Is Erased

U ncle Tito's habit of nibbling cookies carelessly and leaving crumbs everywhere had unpleasant consequences.

I went to the section "Foolish Atoms" to see what books were filed under such a mysterious name, but I didn't manage to read a single title. My hands approached one dark tome, possibly bound in bull hide, when I saw two small antennae. Behind them I saw some legs and behind the legs a brown head. I stood before an insect that made me feel an emptiness in the pit of my stomach. Atop the book, indifferent to my presence, very proud of its slender antennae, stood that most disgusting of creatures: a cockroach.

If spiders interested me, cockroaches made me flee. I ran down a hallway and went through the first door I came across. I kept running until I couldn't run any further and I stopped. My heart pounded in my chest and sweat ran down my face. Naturally, I didn't have the vaguest idea of where I was.

I was about to ring my little bell, but at that moment I encountered what I least wanted to find. Darting across a lettuce-green book, I saw another critter with terrible antennae and scurrying legs. Had I run in a circle and returned to the same place?

Something worse had happened: that cockroach wasn't alone. The entire library was infested.

I fled from there, walking backward to keep my enemies in sight. I backed into a bookcase and various volumes fell to the floor. I didn't stop to pick them up.

I reached a small vestibule, where there was a little table and a chair. An unexpected object sat on the table: a heavy large black telephone, out of another time. I lifted the receiver: there was no dial tone. I hung up and went down a flight of stairs to my right.

That's how I came to the courtyard where Eufrosia did the ironing. I was so concerned by what I had seen that I exclaimed, "We have cockroaches and a telephone!"

"This morning I killed five with a single stomp," the woman told me calmly.

I looked at Eufrosia's large feet, a perfect size for squashing up to twenty of the bugs.

Eufrosia had washed the sheets and hung them out to dry. Seeing them, I was surprised that there were so many. I counted a dozen, even though my bed used only two of them.

"Your uncle hates blankets. He says they weigh too much. He likes to sleep with ten sheets instead. He covers himself with them according to how cold or hot it is. This way he feels like an onion, an 'onion in pajamas.' That's what he says—you know how he likes to say odd things."

"There is a phone in the house!" I exclaimed.

"Your uncle has it for emergencies only. He only connects it if he needs to make a very special call. He hates for it to ring."

Then I heard a voice behind me: "I see you're talking about me."

I turned around. I didn't see him, or rather, I saw only a sheet. My uncle's voice seemed to be coming from the sheet, as if he were a ghost. "I'm sorry for scattering crumbs; it's a bad habit that's a side effect of my enthusiastic but careless way of eating."

"There are cockroaches everywhere!" I told him.

"Yes, I see you lost yourself in Samsa territory."

"What is that?"

"Gregor Samsa was a man who felt like a bug and wound up turning into an insect."

"Did he really exist?"

"No. He was invented by the writer who had the pointiest ears ever. His name was Kafka."

I looked at my uncle's ears. They were rather pointy too. They also had white hairs on them.

"What kind of insect did he turn into?" I asked.

"You mean Kafka? All his life he felt like an insect."

"No, the character."

"Ah, Mr. Samsa. It is one of the great, unsolved mysteries. The writer tells us Mr. Samsa turns into a bug, but provides no more details. Some specialists think that perhaps he was referring to the beetles that live in the wooden beams that are typical of the old houses in Prague, where the story took place. But mankind has very fixed ideas: Kafka wrote 'bug' and everyone thought cockroach, humanity's most repulsive enemy. Now we are invaded. I don't know how many sections of the library already belong to Samsa territory."

"Eufrosia just killed five," I informed him and pointed to her enormous foot.

"This is not something that can be fixed by stomping," my uncle replied, and went out into the yard, looking very upset.

That afternoon, Tito connected the telephone to speak to the fumigator. They had a very heated discussion because the man couldn't come soon enough to satisfy Uncle. The governor had discovered that all the Chinese restaurants were full of rats, and the fumigation company was working non-stop.

"He'll come in a week," Uncle said, with sad resignation. "Meanwhile, we'll resort to guerilla warfare using insecticides."

My uncle's house, which I liked so much despite its making me somewhat nervous, turned into a fearful place. Libraries are places where insects can hide perfectly. If *The Wild Book* was surrounded by cockroaches, I didn't want to find it.

I sprayed insecticide in my bedroom and Eufrosia scattered a poisonous powder that looked like sugar in various corners around the house.

As for my uncle, he produced a flurry of slipper slaps. Holding a book in his left hand, his right was thrust into some thick-soled footwear, and whenever he spied a cockroach, he threw himself at it, as zealous as he was clumsy. It took him ten attempts to hit his target. Most of the time, his rival escaped and he was left on the floor, panting from exhaustion. He didn't resemble my uncle when he was lying on the floor like this; instead he looked like a madman who wore a shoe on his hand.

During the week of the cockroaches, which my uncle baptized as the "Samsa Season," I proposed that we connect the phone.

He was very ashamed of the infestation, so he accepted immediately. "Talk to whomever you want to."

The ideas that occur to us come to us in very strange ways. If someone had asked me a minute ago who I wanted to talk to, I would've said my mother. However, when uncle connected the apparatus, I asked him, "Do you have my dad's number?"

"Your mother gave it to me, in case anything came up. Paris is very far away . . . the call costs more than fumigating cockroaches . . . and besides, it's nighttime there." My uncle didn't seem so eager to appease me anymore.

"You said I could talk to anyone I wanted to."

"That's true, but be brief."

Uncle Tito went to get the little notebook where he had written down my dad's number.

"I've never seen so many numbers all together. I tell you, I detest math."

"We're not going to add or subtract them. We just need to dial them on the phone," I said.

The operation made him so nervous that he dialed various wrong numbers.

Someone in France answered him in a foul mood, and Uncle shouted, "Camembert!" I asked him what that word meant.

"It's the name of a kind of cheese. It was the only thing I could think of. You try dialing, you've got a better grasp of numbers."

I dialed the number and heard my father's firm and joyful voice:

"Juan, what a pleasant surprise!"

I was also surprised to hear him. It felt as if he was so close I could smell his face when he said goodnight to me—a mixture of his lotion and leather—the same smell I had breathed when I slept in his bed.

I was impressed that he knew of so many details pertaining to my life in Uncle's house. He even knew we had cockroaches. He explained that he spoke often with my mother, and she told him everything.

"Your mother and I are very good friends," he told me. "We always will be, even if we won't live together anymore, and we aren't going to stop loving you."

Those words sounded good, but they didn't convince me completely. I wanted him to be with me.

"When are you coming back?" I asked him.

"I'm finishing the bridge. There are still a few more weeks to go."

Was that true? I wanted to ask him many things, but uncle was staring at me with concern: the call was costing a fortune.

"Is it a bridge that splits in two?"

"Yes. In France, there are many rivers with boat traffic. When I get back, we'll go to the movies and to a soccer match. And I'll also buy you a big gift: Napoleon's soldiers."

I wasn't interested in gifts at the moment. What I wanted was for him to be there in the house with us and to help us kill cockroaches.

Despite all that, I was glad to have talked to him after so long.

Then he told me that in France they eat frogs and snails.

"They should come here and eat roaches," I told him, in a bad mood.

Papa asked me to tell him about the plague in the library, and as I told him, little by little, it all started to seem funny. He laughed a lot at my descriptions with that strong laugh of his.

When I told him I was afraid of something, Papa didn't give it any importance. No danger I could tell him about was a good-enough excuse for me to sleep in his bed. He wasn't afraid of monsters or nightmares or cockroaches.

Just then I was overcome by a very confusing feeling. If Papa were there with me, I would have kissed him and I would have hit him. I liked talking to him, but I was also upset that he was so far away. Besides, he hadn't just gone to France to build a bridge. His girlfriend was waiting for him there. I was about to ask him about her, but I was afraid he would ask me about Catalina (it seemed he was aware of so many things, and I didn't want to talk about that).

"It's so good you called, Juan."

I wanted to tell him what I felt but everything was so confusing and he was on the other side of the world, so I answered, "Goodbye, Papa."

When I hung up, Tito looked at me as if I were the head roach of all the cockroaches.

"We've lost a fortune with that phone call!"

"Did you know that the French eat frogs?" I asked him to change the subject.

"You could have found that out for free in a book I have somewhere titled *Disgusting Delicacies*. Besides, young man, the French don't eat the entire frog, just the legs, which taste like chicken. There are very conceited people who disdain roast chicken and think it is very elegant to eat a frog that tastes like chicken. The French are strange, my nephew, but one must accept them: they invented the Rights of Man, and one of them is the right to be insane."

I was about to say to him, "And you practice that right very well," but instead I thought about my father: he was a very specific person, who never got tangled in ideas nor said outlandish things. Just then, I missed him a lot and was glad when Uncle declared, "You need a distraction, my nephew. So long as there are cockroaches, you're not going to be able to search for *The Wild Book*. I'd advise you to go visit the pharmacy. You won't be able to concentrate when confronted by Catalina's loveliness, but you'll be happier."

Tito was right. I could spend hours at the pharmacy, inhaling the delicious scent of medicines, without focusing on anything else but Catalina's honey-colored eyes and her slightly askew tooth.

I explained to her parents that I was there because they were going to fumigate the library. They were very understanding. They gave me a bench to sit on and read, and at five in the afternoon they offered me cookies with milk that were not as good as Eufrosia's, but which I praised highly nonetheless.

I'd brought my book about spiders with me. Reading about other insects made me forget about the cockroaches.

Catalina had a lot of work in those days because there was a flu epidemic and the entire city was sneezing. There were so many sick people coming into the pharmacy that she caught the flu as well. She didn't have a fever, but every now and then she sneezed, with a gentle sound and a magnificent gesture, closing her eyes and wrinkling her nose, as if she had smelled spicy mustard. During those days, I discovered that the things you don't care about or that even bother you in strangers can be nice when you like someone.

From time to time, her mother asked me something about myself. I hadn't told her that my parents were separated, but she treated me with great kindness, as if she suspected something of the sort.

Every third day I spoke to Mama on the phone and she gave me news about Carmen, who was having a fun summer break with her best friend. Papa had told her about our conversation, and she was happy we had spoken.

Mama was becoming a strangely calm person. Although I couldn't be sure, it seemed to me that she no longer smoked (I didn't hear the noise of the match or the pauses when she inhaled the smoke). I, on the other hand, had too many emotions all swirling around inside me.

"You sound a bit strange," Mama told me. "Are you OK?"

I would've liked to tell her that I wanted to see her and that Uncle Tito was a madman surrounded by cockroaches, but I answered only that I was catching a cold and gave a fake cough.

From the pharmacy, I saw the truck of the fumigator finally arrive at Uncle's house. Three men got out. They wore rat-gray uniforms. Each one had a tank on his back, like those used for scuba diving.

They worked in the library for hours and hours. Suddenly, the air in the pharmacy, which had a gentle perfume of gentian and violet, started smelling of something that was poisonous instead of medicinal. Soon I saw the men emerge from Uncle's house. They wore plastic breathing masks over their faces. When they took them off, their expressions showed the utter exhaustion that comes from fighting against resilient and disgusting adversaries. They were such a depressing sight that it was a relief when they got into the truck and drove away from the neighborhood.

When I returned to the library, Uncle shouted, "We need the north wind!"

He had opened all the vents in the house so the smell of poison might go away.

It was hours before it did go away (or perhaps the smell was still there and we had just gotten used to it).

The next day I visited Catalina. Despite her nose being stuffed because of her cold, she told me, "You stink of poison."

She looked paler than usual and had light smudges under her eyes.

"I couldn't sleep all night," she explained, and gave me back the book I had loaned her: *A Discovery on the Heart-Shaped River.*

"Did you like it?" I asked, curious.

"Look at page one hundred and fourteen."

I turned the pages as quickly as I could. I couldn't believe it: the page was blank!

"It's not the only one." Catalina took the book and showed me other blank passages.

I had read the book without finding any blank pages. The book had been erased!

"Could you read the rest?" I asked her.

"I don't dare to say what it's about," she answered.

After I insisted a lot and waited for her to get a customer some sleeping syrup, she told me that our heroes died, drowned in the Heart-Shaped River.

That wasn't what had happened at all! I had read a different story!

What had happened? Until then, she had improved the stories with her reading. Had she lost her power? Was her sickness affecting her in this way? And why were some of the pages erased?

"Whoever wrote this book is a bad person," she said, with a serious tone of voice. "He took away the parts that could be very good and killed the characters with a lot of cruelty. I don't want to know anything more about this river."

"I'm sorry."

"It's not your fault."

"How do you know it's not my fault?"

"The books you read in your uncle's library become different when I read them in the pharmacy. Maybe I've seen so many sick people that the book has caught their sickness."

Catalina was so generous that she took the blame for what she had read. But she couldn't be the cause of the book having been destroyed.

What was going on?

Soon, I would learn that an enemy dwelled in the library that was far more fearsome than the cockroaches.

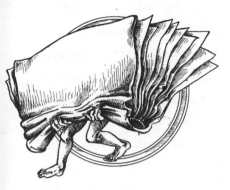

An Enemy

"What you tell me is very strange," Uncle Tito said, as he inspected the book with a magnifying glass.

The convex lens made his right eye, already bulbous, resemble the eye of a puffer fish.

Uncle moved the magnifier. Through it I saw his face; the hairs that stuck out from his nose became gigantic. Then he spoke again, with a voice that was sharp and serious. "It's possible that your friend is not as good a reader as we had thought."

"What do you mean?"

"When you loaned her a book for the first time, she improved it with her reading. There are people who have that ability, but then they lose it. It's beginner's luck. Perhaps she was only interested in impressing you. Your friend worries me, my dear nephew."

"Why is that?"

"It wouldn't be the first time that a great reader, a Princeps reader like yourself, might go off chasing after a pair of pretty eyes and lose their abilities. Catalina has you stupefied and now she's stupefied the book you loaned her."

I didn't like that at all. When she gave the book back to me, Catalina was very worried. She hadn't been able to sleep all night. The book had become strange for another reason: it had turned against the two of us.

But Uncle thought differently. He walked around the room in great strides. Then he stopped, crossed his arms, and said, "I once had a friend who was a genius at reading. Universities fought for his brains. One of those prodigies that humanity produces every hundred years. And one day he fell in love with a student, married her, and decided to grow vegetables."

"And was he happy?" I asked.

"What does that matter? Don't you realize what a waste it is to have a genius growing carrots?"

It seemed to me that it was better to be happy than to be a genius, but I didn't say anything because Uncle was so worked up that he looked like he was about to start breathing fire.

After a long moment of silence, and now much more calmly, he continued, "Books propose problems and the obligation of a wise person is to confront them. No matter how complicated or uncomfortable an idea may be, they will value it. Beekeepers don't complain that their bees have

112

stingers. The same thing happens with someone wise: they must care for a hive of ideas, even if some sting and others are venomous."

I didn't dare take my eyes off this man with hairs in his nostrils who approached while saying, "Even if the ideas are a wasp's nest or an anthill, we must confront them. They can buzz like mad and have that ugly look of critters with too many legs, but one must allow them to live. My friend gave up: he spent his best years planting vegetables in the company of a lovely young woman, who over time turned into an interesting lady, I can't deny that."

"You said you had a friend who grew broccoli and also invented things," I reminded him.

"This is different. I'm all for people having hobbies, as long as they don't interfere with the development of knowledge. What interests you more, Catalina or the books?"

I was upset he'd asked me that. He didn't know Catalina or how much she had suffered because of the destruction of the story about the river. At that moment, my relative reminded me of a bitter old man who had spent too much time alone and didn't know how to appreciate people.

I refused to answer.

He crossed the room in five long strides, trying to calm down. When he spoke again, however, his voice still trembled with fury. "She ruined the book you loaned her! She doesn't deserve for you to keep lending her books to read."

Those words made me so angry that I immediately left the room.

At dinnertime, uncle wanted to get back in my good graces. "I understand that you like Catalina, Nephew. I too was once young, although that might seem impossible to you."

I didn't answer.

"But I don't want you to get too distracted and lose your reading powers. We could find *The Wild Book*!"

I took a bite of cake that tasted horrible to me. Uncle looked at me through a cloud of smoky tea. Then he repeated the question that he had asked me this morning, but this time asked it more aggressively, as if he now belonged to the Mafia. "If you had to give up books to be with Catalina, what would you do?"

I didn't answer him this time, but he knew what my answer would be: I would prefer to be with Catalina than read books and remain alone like my uncle.

"I know what you're thinking," my disgruntled relative said. "You would rather be with Catalina than to read books and be alone like your uncle."

It was as if he had read my mind.

"I was right, wasn't I?" he asked, very satisfied with himself.

I still didn't say anything.

Uncle stood up from the table. "That's the proof that Catalina has you in her power."

Although my uncle's words bothered me, what he had said was true: I cared much more about Catalina than anything else.

Was that bad? I couldn't believe that she would want anything bad for me.

"She is an intruder," Uncle said from the door to the kitchen. "She lives across the street from us, but it's as if she has snuck into this house. She is driving us apart. She is meddlesome. Be careful, my nephew."

And with those hideous words, my uncle left me in the kitchen, facing a cake that tasted increasingly worse with every bite I took.

That night I couldn't sleep. I was furious with Uncle Tito. Well, in reality I was furious with all adults. First my father left, then my mother sent me to live with a relative we almost never saw, and now Uncle had gone mad. He was an original, that was unquestionable, but the ideas that occurred to him were strange and useless.

I spent several hours tossing and turning in bed. I wouldn't even have minded dreaming about the scarlet room if that meant I could finally fall asleep.

It was the early hours of the morning when I heard a door open somewhere else in the house. Perhaps Uncle was also awake.

Since I had drenched the sheets in sweat from so much tossing and turning, I decided to go for a walk.

I went down a hallway that seemed to be longer and lonelier than usual, until I heard a faint noise that sounded like someone was opening and closing books or rubbing sheets of paper together.

Not far from where I was, the hallway turned and led to a room full of maps where Uncle liked to read. I headed there. As I advanced, the noises became louder.

The door to the map room was ajar. I didn't have to push it open to see Uncle at his desk, concentrating as he read from a blue book. His right eyebrow rose in a zigzag and his forehead wrinkled into three deep lines. His face looked malevolent. If it were possible to guess what he was reading by the expression on his face, I would say he was reading a treatise on black magic.

Just then I felt something furry touch my bare feet. Luckily, it was only Domino, my favorite cat. He circled my legs, hoping I would pet his side. I picked him up because I liked to hear his purring, and then something occurred to me. I took the bell, which I carried with me everywhere, tied it to Domino's tail, and put him down in the hallway. The cat started to run, making a sharp tinkling.

Uncle Tito lifted his head, with that expression of frustration that interruptions always provoked in him, adjusted his glasses to be able to see into the distance, and decided to check out what was going on. He must've thought I had gotten lost in some corner of his enormous library.

He headed toward the door. I pulled some books out of the lowest shelf and hid myself in their place.

Uncle tripped on the books I left in the hallway, but he didn't lose his balance and kept going, muttering something about Eufrosia not being able to keep the house in order.

The bell tinkled in the distance.

I took advantage of Uncle's absence to approach his desk and examine the book he was reading.

I was surprised by the thickness of the paper. It seemed to be made of vellum. Right then I wouldn't have been surprised to find out that the pages were made from human skin.

The pages had been written in black ink and one could see the brushstrokes. I marked Uncle's page with a goose feather.

I closed the heavy Blue Book. Uncle had told me that it was written in Latin. However, I could read the title without problems:

The Book of Bibliodivination
OPEN IT AT RANDOM,
IF YOU DARE

I returned to the page Uncle was on. The last line had a very strange sentence: *Redurtni eht ot dne na tup tsum uoy.*

What did that mean? Was it a key in Latin?

I heard the bell in the distance, a good sign: Uncle had not yet caught Domino.

I went over the sentence various times. The book asked to be opened at random. If I tried it, would the message it offered me be clear? I let the volume fall open at a different page. On the last line, I found another incomprehensible phrase: *Wodahs ruoy morf eelf.*

I looked for a dictionary on the table. As I rifled through the books and many papers that populated the desk, I stumbled upon something strange—a mirror.

I opened the book to the page uncle had been on. The words reordered themselves when reflected by the mirror. The first sentence read, "You must put an end to the intruder."

That was the sentence uncle had studied with his eyebrow in a zigzag! The book had sided against Catalina! It was a malignant text. Only that could explain his change in attitude. Tito had said books are mirrors that reflect what we are. That book was a mirror of another kind: it reflected false things that caused damage.

Then I used the mirror to read the sentence from my own page: "Flee from your shadow." What did that mean?

That's when I heard a shout, "Dang it, Domino!"

Uncle had caught the cat. I heard his steps as he returned toward the room. I took the book and went out into the hallway.

I didn't pause to think about what I was doing. The only thing I wanted was for Uncle not to find me there.

I ran as fast as I could toward a staircase. I went up it in leaps and bounds. The book was very large and heavy and hindered my movements.

I reached the upstairs floor, fearful of having made a betraying sound. I tried to tiptoe but the book began to weigh more with each step, as if it didn't like that I was carrying it or didn't like where we were going. Only then did I remember that I was near the books for the blind that my great-uncle used to read.

I sat down in the hallway to reflect. The Blue Book had given me advice: "Flee from your shadow." That was very strange. Nobody can flee from their own shadow, it's something that belongs to you and moves with you. That would be like fleeing from yourself. Besides, if the book advised me to do something, I should do the opposite. I couldn't let it bespell me as it had Uncle. I should stay close to my shadow. And more importantly, I had friends in the shadows.

I decided to carry the book of terrible riddles to the room of the books for the blind.

As I approached the door, the weight in my arms became unbearable. I put the book on the floor to open the door and could barely manage to lift it up again. I felt like my fingers were going to break under the weight of those pages that had turned into iron, but with great effort I managed to pick it up again.

I entered the room and the door closed behind me. This time I didn't feel even slightly afraid. This room held the books that had helpfully arranged themselves into steps to allow me to escape. Suddenly, not only could I carry the book easily, but I also felt flooded with relief.

I walked toward a bookcase and placed the book on a shelf. It immediately fell to the floor. Three or four books fell on top of it, as if they were trying to disable it. Yes, I had allies here, unknown friends who lived in books that I couldn't read, but who were willing to help me. Perhaps that's why, in my solitary games as a child, I had imagined the Shadow Club.

I returned to the door easily. The room was dark, but I oriented myself with strange surety, as if I were walking in a dream.

I heard sounds from the floor below. Uncle was searching for something on his desk.

I knew what it was. I also knew he wasn't going to find it.

The Pirate Book

Although this story took place many years ago now, I haven't forgotten the sound that shook Uncle Tito's house the next day. It was something as strange as if a horse had neighed in the living room.

Those rooms in which one usually only heard the turning of pages or the gentle pitter-patter of the cats were altered by a sound that nobody could expect. To the surprise of us all, the phone rang!

Uncle answered and I ran to him to be able to hear his responses.

"Carmen? Here? Why?"

When I reached the little table where the phone rested, he had already hung up. He looked down at the rug thoughtfully.

When he noticed my presence, he looked up and said, "Your sister is coming to spend a few days with us."

He looked very worried. His face was no longer the threatening sight it had been the previous night.

He approached me and tried to caress my hair with his plate-drying movement. He was once again my usual uncle, a bit strange, but nice enough all in all.

"I want to beg for your forgiveness, Nephew," he said suddenly.

"Why?"

"I insulted your girlfriend."

"Catalina is not my girlfriend!" I shouted, although, truth be told, I felt an odd sense of pride that Uncle thought she was.

"Whatever she is!" he said. "I'm sorry, I don't know what's happening to me. Lately, I get irritable more than usual. Perhaps I'm drinking too much of my smoky tea."

"What were you saying about my sister?"

"Oh, yes! She was spending the holiday at a friend's house. Her name is Leila Bermúdez."

"I know that. What happened?"

"Her friend's father was offered a job in the US. They're moving in a few days. Carmen will spend the rest of her break with us. Does she like stuffed toys?"

"Yes."

"And does she have a lot of them?"

"Lots and lots."

"And is she going to bring them with her?" Uncle asked strange questions.

"Perhaps she'll bring Juanito."

"She has a toy with the same name as you?"

"She named it that so I would invite her to the Shadow Club."

"What's that?" Uncle was very interested.

"I made up a story of a secret club that meets to go on nighttime adventures. I told Carmen to make her jealous and she believed everything. She always believes me."

"It's curious, very curious," Uncle said, scratching his chin.

"I don't understand."

"A few days ago, you went into the room of the books for the blind. They helped you to leave, forming steps and placing themselves beneath your feet. I have already told you that some of the best readers have been blind. My father stopped seeing at a very young age. Your great-grandfather was also blind. He founded this library. You have a very peculiar association with the Shadow Books."

Tito paused. He ran his fingers over his unshaved chin, making a rasping sound. He squeezed his chin, as if he wanted to make ideas spurt from it. Finally, he said, "Something very strange happened last night."

Had he discovered what I'd done? Did he know I had carried the malignant book to the room with the Shadow Books? Wanting to change the subject, I asked, "Why were you interested in my sister's stuffed animals?"

"A long time ago a child entered this house with a toy rabbit. Eufrosia brought him here. He was her nephew; he came from her village and his parents left him here for a few hours. His pet seemed an innocent stuffed rabbit, but it had a fungus that really likes paper. My entire library was infected! Thousands and thousands of books from all eras were in danger. That fearsome stuffed rabbit had been in contact with sick books. The boy was an altar boy in Eufrosia's village. In the village church, the priest had ancient books that would have been of incalculable value had they been clean. But they were books with a fungus that eats at your skin. Look at these marks!" Uncle stretched his wrists toward me, showing me whitish stripes I hadn't seen before. "The fungi striped my skin! They would have left me like a Bengal tiger if I hadn't fumigated all those books, page by page. No specialist wanted to do it because they were afraid of spending so much time in contact with the fungus. I had to scatter the powder personally. For two years I didn't read a single line, I just cured sick books. It was the worst time in my life. This library became a hospital for dying pages. The air smelled of toxic substances and Eufrosia stopped coming. I lived on bread and water, like a prisoner. And do you want to know the most tragic part?"

"Didn't breathing so much poison affect you?" I asked.

"What do you think?" Uncle smiled in a strange way. "Do I seem a little odd to you?"

"The truth is that you do," I dared to say.

"I've always been like this! I'm not interested in being a boring and normal person."

"There's nothing bad about being normal."

"It seems boring to me. A toaster is normal. On the other hand, a tasty stew is special. I prefer to be a stew."

"You're my uncle, not something to eat."

"It all depends on how anthropophagous you are. There are cannibals who have snacked on their favorite uncles."

"I'm only saying that it's not bad for us to be normal."

"Don't pretend you're not extraordinary. You might look thoroughly normal—two eyes, one nose, and an unremarkable belly—but you've got the ability to attract the best of books to you. You are a Lector Princeps, and no one can take that away from you. That's why I need you. The poison didn't affect me, dear nephew. What affected me was the loneliness and not knowing what to do with so much reading. You can change that. I only hope your sister's stuffed animals don't have any fungi."

"They haven't been in contact with old books."

"I still haven't recovered from that rabbit that was so contagious. Books are living beings. One must take great care of them. I'm going to confess something: last night I made a grave error."

"What do you mean?" I asked as innocently as I could.

"Do you remember that book I ordered, the one with a blue cover that is very old?"

"More or less," I lied.

"I told you it was a book to look for other books."

"Oh, yes, I remember something. Didn't you mention that it was an explorer book?"

"In reality, it's a Pirate Book."

"Pirate?"

"People call the books that are made without permission, the badly made copies that are sold on the street 'Pirate Books.' But there's another kind of Pirate Book: one that intercepts the messages of other books and robs them so nobody can read them. That is what happened with the book you loaned Catalina. Now I know."

"Tell me," I said, very interested.

"I wanted to see what you were reading and I made the mistake of leaving *A Discovery on the Heart-Shaped River* next to the Blue Book, and it stole the contents! You gave the book to Catalina the next morning. It was already altered."

"How could that happen?"

"Books have contact among themselves; some of them make friends, others even seem relatives. But there are also some jealous ones that despise the good messages of others and try and hurt them. They are books made by people who are unable to create something on their own, and who can only destroy what others make. That's what the Blue Book is. I thought it would help me to find *The Wild Book*. Great specialists spoke wonders of that treatise of divination, but there are also specialists who make mistakes or who have bad intentions. Not everything that is written is good, my dear nephew."

Uncle paused. He gasped as if he were coming up for air from under the water. Then he went on, "That Blue Book is the worst of the Pirate Books, made to loot and damage other books. The author didn't sign it with his name. He is a coward who hides. Whoever wrote it hates all other writers. He wanted to be the only author on the Earth. That's why he wants to put an end to all others, especially the good ones, who make him the angriest. I should've known this, but my ambition to obtain a very special book got the better of me. Yesterday, I looked at you with fury and jealousy. I recognize this and ask for your forgiveness. It was as if I were drugged. I hated you and I hated your friend because you both are able to read as I am not able to, by improving the story. The book advised me to separate you from Catalina, and didn't stop there with its terrible advice."

"What else did it say?"

"I'll tell you everything, but promise me first that you'll forgive me."

"Don't worry," I said with a trembling voice.

"I'm not a Lector Princeps, I've never been one. I can detect who is, but I don't have your powers. I wanted to find *The Wild Book* on my own and that's why I resorted to that terrible, blue-covered treatise. Instead of letting you do everything, I wanted to get ahead of you, using a book that turned out to be an enemy."

I saw that Tito hadn't touched his mug of tea. I'd never seen him speak for so long without drinking or going to the bathroom.

"Before you came I was very sad," he continued. "I thought I would die without deciphering the mystery of this library. My father spoke to me of *The Wild Book*, but that volume hasn't wanted me to read it. It is like a stallion that doesn't accept a rider, or rather one that awaits a very special rider. I thought that there was no solution. Anguished, I went to the section of books on magic and learned about this ancient treatise for divination. It was recommended by some famous, supposedly wise men, but now I know they're bad. Evil, my dear nephew, doesn't always seem to be bad. Sometimes it even seems good. I ordered the book before you arrived. I didn't know that I'd have the opportunity to turn to you for help. When the malevolent book arrived, you were already here. You saw it come in. I should've gotten rid of it, but the temptation was too strong. Its pages took me over. I lost control. I was stunned. I sunk into those pages like a tea bag in boiling water. I was completely submerged. Only now am I your uncle once more. This morning I woke up feeling completely different."

"Different from when?" I asked, trying to follow what he was saying.

"From yesterday. During the night, the book disappeared from my desk. I was insanely furious and looked for it everywhere, with special flashlights and growing desperation. I couldn't find it. Curiously, I awoke much calmer, with my mind cleared. Now I understand that it was good for me to separate myself from that book. That's why I can now see things in another light and ask for your forgiveness. Do you forgive me?"

"I already forgave you, Uncle," I answered, embarrassed by such insistence.

"Do you know why I connected the telephone?" he asked me.

"So my mother could call?"

"Of course not. To ask for advice from the rector of the university. He's an old friend of mine. I wanted to warn him that I had an enemy of books in my home. I needed advice to locate it."

"Isn't it better for it to remain lost?" I asked, feigning innocence.

"It's good that it's lost, but I'm afraid that it will turn up again. I need to know how to confront it."

"And was the rector able to help you?"

"He is a great expert on evil books. Unfortunately, he has too much work. I spoke to him a while ago but he couldn't talk: he had a meeting with the coach for the university's football team, which is about to drop down to the second division. I suppose that's more important to him than a pirate book. We said we would talk when his sports problem had been resolved. That's why I left the telephone connected, and that's why your mother's call came in; she tried it on the off chance that she would get through. This business with your sister is an emergency. I wonder how many emergencies can fit in this house . . . "

"And isn't there any way of controlling the Blue Book?"

"Certain books are so powerful that they can annul a Pirate Book. They subdue it and eliminate its effects. It's possible that there are some books in this house that are strong enough, but I don't know how to find them."

Then I summoned up my courage and I asked him, "Can I tell you something and will you promise not to get upset?"

"Of course, Nephew, I am so ashamed at my conduct yesterday. I am not going to get mad at you. You already forgave me, and now I will forgive any of your defects, be they small, medium, or large."

I took a deep breath and told him in a rush what had happened the night before.

Uncle looked at me, without losing his smile. "Then you put the bell on Domino? I should have suspected. What use are my brains? I was so affected by that evil book that I acted like a fool. Your solution was magnificent. The jealous book has been controlled by the Shadow Books, which it can't read. How wonderful that you're with me! We can disconnect the phone!"

"What if the rector calls?"

"That doesn't matter. This emergency is over."

Uncle leaned forward to unplug the machine.

"Don't you feel a curious serenity? What a ruckus the telephone makes."

 "It only rang once."

"And that seems little to you? For me it was the equivalent of a cannonball. It will be a long time before I recover." He lifted his tea to his lips and exclaimed, "Buah! This is the first time a cup of tea has gone cold on me. I've never spoken for so long without sipping on my precious herbs. Let's go to the kitchen, my dear nephew: we need to recover our strength."

And thus ended the long dialogue with my relative, who, to the books' and to my own good fortune, had once again returned to normal.

The Prince Makes the Rules

Uncle Tito spent the following days in a great mood. He sent Eufrosia to the store to buy things for special stews and he hummed strange songs while he repaired his books.

He also took me to the statue room to show me the corner that I hadn't noticed before.

I liked looking over those framed photographs. There weren't many—perhaps only twenty. I looked at the faces of people from other times, who I didn't know but without whom I wouldn't exist.

"Your family," Uncle said.

"I don't recognize anyone," I answered.

"You lack practice in comparing noses and eyebrows. I don't recognize faces well either. I'm not very sentimental and I almost never look at these photos. But sometimes

I come here to remember that I have relatives. Some are very distant or are connected to the family by marriage, but I like to look at them. I have a collector's soul, and I like to collect even relatives. Since I'm not very social, I prefer to see them in photographs, without hearing them snore, sneeze, or blow their noses."

My attention was caught by a photo of a boy of around eight and I asked who it was.

"You won't believe it: that's your father!"

"That boy?"

"Look closely, Nephew, he has the face of a future engineer. His eyes look into the distance, as if he were trying to construct a bridge."

I peered at the somewhat chubby face of the boy who many years later would become my dad.

"You have the same spot on your cheek, the same forehead, identical eyebrows. You look just like one another," Uncle commented.

It was true that there was a strong resemblance between us. He could've been my younger brother.

"What are you thinking?" Uncle asked me.

"How do you know I'm thinking something?"

"You've got a look that isn't quite like an engineer's. You're different from your father in that. Your eyes are on the lookout for mysteries. They're the eyes of a detective of people, that is to say, the eyes of a Lector Princeps."

"I felt something strange: I felt older than my own dad!"

"You're growing, Juan. You now have your own life. Perhaps you haven't realized it, but you've been making many decisions on your own. You need your parents and they need you; but, you also have your own path. Your father was once the boy in that photo. You could give advice to that boy; you know more now than he knew then. Time passes in an incredible way. One day you'll be the one who takes care of your parents, and I hope you have some extra time to take care of your uncle."

I scanned the other photographs until I found one of a girl sleeping in a field. The sun was shining on her face and she smiled, as if she were enjoying a siesta after a tasty picnic.

Uncle explained that it was a photograph of my mother when she was sixteen. She looked very calm and beautiful. I would have loved to play in that field with her.

We spent a long while talking about the beards and hairstyles of other relatives. Then I felt an urgent desire to go to the pharmacy and speak with Mama.

I crossed the street, greeted Catalina quickly, and dialed the number I already knew by heart.

I told Mama that I had seen pictures of her and of Papa when they were young.

"You look a lot like your father," she said.

"But bigger," I joked.

I asked after my sister, and she told me that in a few days she'd bring Carmen over to us.

My mother sounded calm and relaxed. She encouraged me to keep reading and enjoying being at Uncle's house.

"Are you taking your iron?"

"I no longer need it," I said, with such certainty that she didn't add anything more.

After hanging up I went to the counter to tell Catalina the big news: she wasn't the one who had ruined the adventure on the Heart-Shaped River; it had been the Blue Book. I told her everything, in full detail.

Catalina's smiles were overwhelming. "It wasn't my fault!" she cried.

Then I understood how useful it is sometimes to have an enemy. The Blue Book brought us together again. We would fight against it to keep the other books safe.

Catalina suggested we continue looking for more stories about the river, and I went back to the house, happier than ever.

I found my relative in a good but somewhat pensive mood. "The moment has come to acknowledge that I am defeated, Nephew," he told me.

"What do you mean?"

"You are one Lapsang Souchong away from becoming my boss."

"I don't understand."

"Be patient; battles aren't won in an instant."

Having said that, he went into the kitchen and returned with a steaming cup. Despite the fact that the liquid was boiling hot, he drank it in almost one gulp. Then he said,

"You've shown to have great affinity with the books. Now I understand my mission: to provide support, to be your squire. The books prefer you."

He drank what remained of his tea in one lip-smacking gulp. Then he ran the back of his hand over his mouth and exclaimed, "Aaaahhhh!"

Life with only books for company didn't result in good manners. I didn't much care if someone was dirty or noisy when they ate, but Uncle almost set records. Before he spoke again, he burped loudly, stuck a finger in his ear, discovered a crumb, and ate it as if it were the most delicious sweet. He had the table manners of a rodent.

These gestures didn't seem to indicate excitement, but Uncle, or so he said, was indeed going through a situation that moved him greatly. This is what he told me:

"I never thought that someone would come to be more important to me than myself. You don't know how much I appreciate that you're here with me. You are the guide I needed."

Anyone else would have worn a face of import or would have spoken in a voice choked with emotion. Instead, Uncle discovered more crumbs, got down on his hands and knees, ate the ones he could reach, and sniffed the ground to see if he discovered any further traces of food. Then he returned to me, like a bloodhound that had suddenly found its owner's tracks.

"Don't you have anything to say?"

"Thanks."

"Is that all?"

"I can't think of anything else," I confessed.

"For the new guide of this magnificent library, you seem rather simple."

Uncle walked on his knees toward me.

"Libraries suffer from sicknesses, Nephew: fungi, moths, termites, cockroaches, mice. But there is yet another plague that threatens them—one that can't be fought with fumigation."

He stood up at last and said, "Arrogance is worse than roaches. I thought I knew too much and that stupid book turned me against you. There is nothing worse than someone who isn't aware of their own ignorance."

"I don't understand."

"You see?" he said, enthusiastically. "You're honest. When you don't know something, you say so. Many people pretend to know more than they do. You are sincere. The moment has come for you to take the lead and decide what we should do."

"Me?"

"You are a Lector Princeps!"

"I've read less than you have."

"Intuition at work is worth more than knowledge."

"How do you know my intuition works?"

"I don't know it, the books do. That is what matters."

I was about to say something, but just then I turned my head toward the room's table and was surprised to discover a book with an extraordinary title: *A Friend on the Heart-Shaped River.*

"Do you see what I mean?" uncle said with astonishment. The book had arrived there on its own, without our seeing it do so.

"Books search for their readers. You are a Lector Princeps, and the prince makes the rules. Tell me what we should do."

He placed one knee on the ground. I thought he was looking for another crumb, but then he said to me, with great seriousness, "Place one hand on my shoulder and name me your squire. It is an old custom of knights."

I did as he requested.

"I will obey you to the death, prince of the books," he said in a deep voice.

I felt a strange trembling as I placed my hand on his shoulder, as if I were being charged with energy.

Uncle looked at me with his bulging eyes. "What shall we do, milord?" He seemed very enthusiastic to be a squire.

"Before anything else, call me Juan. I am your nephew and you're my uncle."

"Some squires have also been uncles. I accept the charge. What direction shall we take?"

My uncle's exaggerated servility made me uncomfortable. That's why I said, "Go to the kitchen."

"To the kitchen? And where will you go?"

"To the library."

"Alone?"

"I'll take Domino."

"Don't forget your bell," Uncle reminded me.

That gave me an idea.

"I want to give it back to you." I placed the small bell on top of the table. "I can now orient myself alone in the library."

"Are you sure?"

"'The prince makes the rules,'" I reminded him.

"That's fine, milord . . . I mean, Nephew Juan."

The truth is that I wasn't very sure that I knew the labyrinth of rooms and hallways by heart, but the moment had come to show that I could lead.

I felt curiously free as I explored the library without the little bell.

I went to the section "How to Exit the Labyrinth." I wanted to find books related to the library; books that could show me new paths to try.

I got lost a few times, but managed to find my way again. Finally, I reached the shelves filled with books that dealt with disorientation strategies. I read about physical labyrinths (made of bricks in homes and cities, or from plants in forests and gardens), and also of mental labyrinths that employ tricks to mislead and confuse the brain.

I was surprised by how many tactics there were to confuse people. Curiously, the section was called "How to

Exit the Labyrinth." I say "curiously" because for nearly the entire day I only found descriptions of labyrinths without finding any instructions for exiting them.

I was so interested in the subject that I forgot to eat. I read standing up and then seated on the floor. I found out about families who had lived for various generations without knowing any other landscape than that of a labyrinth.

Suddenly, I realized I'd been so caught up in my reading that I hadn't looked at my watch all day. It was midnight! Uncle must be worried, I thought. I decided to go back. But then a title caught my attention: *A Clock of Letters*. The first sentence was: "All times are in this one."

The book was about labyrinths of time. I flipped through it quickly because I wanted to get back to Uncle. Although I only spent a few moments looking at those pages, their effect on me was powerful. In an instant, I remembered things that seemed very distant. I thought of my first tricycle, of the toys my dad used to make for me, of the taste of a pistachio ice cream I hadn't ever tasted again, of the day Mama forgot to come pick us up at school and we had to walk home, of the way she hugged us and I breathed in the smell of her hair. How distant that all seemed! And at the same time, how near! The book made me feel that these memories lived powerfully within me. I put it back in its place.

Then something incredibly strange happened: beside it I saw a white book, without any printed letters. It seemed a half-made volume, its spine made from an untreated, somewhat scratchy fabric. Had it been put there carelessly or by accident? But now wasn't the moment to wonder what kind of book it could be: I had to grab it!

I tried to pick it up but it slipped between my fingers. It was as fast as lightning—so fast I couldn't see it move. It simply stopped being there. I barely managed to brush it with the tips of my fingers. My hand tingled, thrilled, as if it had a mind of its own.

The other books closed ranks to hide it. There was no gap on the shelf, as if that book had never been there.

I heard a bell—Uncle had come to look for me.

"I've been searching the library for hours," he exclaimed when he saw me. "Dinner has gone cold."

Then I said, "I touched it."

Uncle was still thinking about food, so it took him a while to react. Suddenly he lifted his head and asked, "You touched what?"

"I touched it!" I couldn't say anything else, and I couldn't stop looking at my hand. Finally, I managed to say, "I saw it. It's white and has no letters. It looks like a book that isn't finished."

"*The Wild Book*," Uncle murmured.

"It escaped."

"It must be tamed for it to return."

"How?"

"You'll discover the way. I am just your humble squire."

Only then did I notice the smell of food. Uncle opened his right hand. "I brought you a sandwich for the journey."

The bread had turned into a handful of crumbs in Uncle's fist.

"I was very nervous when I couldn't find you and I squeezed the sandwich too hard."

I tried a few crumbs. Although it looked inedible, it tasted yummy.

I memorized the place where I had brushed the white book and I set about eating my dinner as if it were the first meal of my life.

Tito Cooks Novels

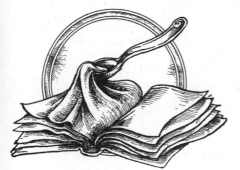

The next day I woke up late, tired after the many hours I had spent in the library. I decided to stay in bed. I imagined I lived in Australia as a happy platypus. The platypus, one of my favorite animals, could spend long periods of time without moving. It would have been even better to have been a kangaroo. A small kangaroo that rests in its mother's pouch. But one can't have everything in life; I had already decided to imagine I was a platypus, and that's how I spent the better part of the morning.

The always-cheerful Eufrosia brought me the book I had left in the living room: *A Friend on the Heart-Shaped River.*

I spent hours reading and anticipating the pleasure of taking the book to Catalina. I liked its adventure more and more. This time, the main characters found a boy lost in the forest who didn't know anything about the outdoors. They weren't as knowledgeable as Eagle Eye, but they already knew the secrets of fire making and they could differentiate among the tracks of a wide variety of animals. The other boy was named Bruno and wore a very colorful vest because he belonged to a youth chorus. He had come to the forest in the strangest way.

He studied in a school for singers that only accepted students with magnificent voices. That summer, his class had taken a boat to give a performance in the north of the country. Every two days they stopped at a site of interest. After visiting the great lakes of the region, they took a trip through the forest. Bruno wasn't very athletic and fell behind. It was hard work for him to climb the hills and move through the underbrush. He began to despair of ever reaching the others, and as he leaped from one rock to the next, his glasses fell into a crevice. From that moment onwards, the landscape became a blur through which he walked aimlessly until night fell and he knew he was lost.

Ernesto and Marina found the very frightened boy the next day. Bruno was good at math and had a wonderful voice that was especially well suited to sing Christmas songs. But those skills were of little use in a place where one had to defend oneself against wolves and know which way the wind blew so as not to provoke a forest fire when lighting a campfire.

Bruno wasn't especially friendly. He was afraid of bugs and anything that looked sticky, or even just dirty. Since he couldn't see well, every now and then he'd stick his foot in an anthill or step on a pile of dung. Ernesto and Marina had to take care of him as if he were their younger sibling.

He proved to be too immature for life in the forest. Until that trip, he had only ever seen food in the refrigerator of his house. He didn't know how to hunt or fish or harvest fruit. He only knew how to open boxes of cereal or cans of tuna.

While Ernesto and Marina took care of Bruno, the ship of singing children continued on its journey. The concert they were to give was very important, and the director of the chorus had decided that twenty-nine children could sing just as well as thirty. At the next port, the authorities were informed that one of the children had remained behind in the forest and were asked to go find him.

Various helicopters overflew the region in search of Bruno. Although he wore a vest of many colors, it couldn't be seen through the thick canopy of the trees. The helicopters searched the forest for days without finding the lost boy.

The clumsy and fearful boy let Ernesto and Marina put into practice the many things they knew. Since the new boy didn't know anything, they had to teach him how to salt meat to preserve it and how to distinguish the song of an owl from that of a nightingale.

Explaining things makes one appreciate how much one knows. Bruno made Ernesto and Marina realize all that they had learned in the forest.

Little by little, Bruno began to take advantage of his musical ear to recognize birdsongs and to imitate them with such precision that all sorts of birds were summoned when he sang.

In the last chapter, Ernesto and Marina took Bruno to the place where the river merged in the shape of a heart. There they asked the singing boy to imitate the sounds of the birds, and an enormous congregation of birds gathered in the skies. This spectacle drew the attention of the helicopters, who had not yet lost hope of finding Bruno.

I didn't get out of bed until I had finished the book. Then I got dressed as fast as I could and went to the pharmacy.

I didn't find Catalina. She had gone out to take some pills to someone's home, for the messenger was also out sick.

Her mother was behind the counter.

I handed her *A Friend on the Heart-Shaped River* and asked her to give it to Catalina.

The woman spoke to me in a friendly but firm tone. "I don't know if I should give it to her. All this reading has left her very tired. I've forbidden her to read at night but she keeps reading in secret. Reading is good, but you two take it to an extreme."

"It's just a book," I protested.

Catalina's mother gave me a curious look. "A book is never just a book. You know that better than anyone."

She was right. I didn't know what to say.

"I'm worried that Catalina will get upset like last time," she commented. "She got dark patches under her eyes and I even heard her cry."

"This book is a good one, and it'll be even better when she reads it."

She seemed to remember something, and she looked at me with more sympathy.

"Many years ago, Cata's father gave me a marvelous book." Her eyes lit up. "It also had the word 'heart' in the title. It was a book about medicine, but it seemed very romantic to me."

"Will you give her the book?" I asked hopefully.

"I'll see how I feel. That's all I can promise you."

With those words, I left the pharmacy.

I began to wonder if I would ever find *The Wild Book*. What could I do? The library surpassed my powers. What's more, the book we were looking for hadn't wanted to be read by anyone. It was a rebel. Like the final combatant of an army that took refuge in the mountains and never surrendered. Was it worth searching for? The library was impossible for a single person to cope with.

I remembered what I had read in *A Friend on the Heart-Shaped River*. There are some things that are very difficult to do when one is alone and very pleasant to do in the right company. Ernesto and Marina faced challenges that demanded lots of courage and strength, but then relived them enthusiastically when they remembered them by the heat of the campfire. The best part of their adventures was that they had been shared with someone. I decided to invite Catalina to the library. I couldn't do it without Uncle's permission, so I went to look for him in the reading room, but I didn't find him. He wasn't in the fern room either, or in the map room, where he generally enclosed himself for hours on end.

After a while I saw Obsidian and Ivory heading toward the kitchen, as if they had smelled something delicious. I followed them and found Uncle standing there all covered in flour.

"I'm breading a fish à la Moby Dick."

The cats watched him attentively, awaiting the results. Soon, Domino also appeared.

I wanted to talk with my uncle, but he was in no mood for interruptions. He bit his tongue so as not to lose his focus, and every now and then he paged through a thick book. I thought it was a book of recipes and was surprised to learn that it was a novel instead.

"What are you looking for in there?" I asked him.

"Herman Melville wrote a magnificent adventure on the foamy seas. I want to make food that tastes like novels. Moby Dick is the name of a white whale. There isn't enough room in this humble kitchen to cook whales, so I settled for trying to cook one of the salmon it had in its belly. The secret is to shake it a lot. You mustn't think it's smooth sailing in the belly of a whale, especially one as aggressive as Moby Dick. The final touch is the harpoon of taste."

Uncle took a sewing needle and plunged it into a plate overflowing with sauce. Then he stuck it in the fish until he'd pierced it through completely, and continued to explain his strange recipe. "Captain Ahab was furious with Moby Dick because he'd eaten off one of his legs in a single bite. For the whale that was a simple snack, like a sea sausage. The captain hated the whale and wanted to kill it, even if he died in the attempt. He searched for the whale in the most dangerous oceans until he finally found it and was able to look the behemoth in its terrible eye. Moby Dick had survived many harpoons, and some were even stuck in its thick skin. The creature was so large that the harpoons looked like tiny corkscrews impaled in its scar-covered body. Ahab's final harpoon thrust pierced the whale. The white beast got so upset that it destroyed the ship and the entire crew. Only one sailor was saved: Ishmael, who then tells us the story. Whatever happens, there is always a witness so the world can learn the story. Fish à la Moby Dick would be nothing without the Ishmael sauce." Uncle pointed to the plate of sauce where he had sunk the needle.

"What's the sauce made from?" I asked.

"I can't reveal my recipe. We chefs are interested in what goes into the mouth, not what comes out of it. The chef swallows his secrets. I'll only tell you one thing: sailors like tattoos. This sauce is so tasty it's unforgettable. It's as if it leaves a tattoo of deliciousness on the inside of your stomach."

Uncle's fantastical way of reading was now manifesting in his cooking. It was very difficult to change the subject. At last, I managed to ask him, "Can I invite Catalina?"

"To the movies? That's fine. You have my permission. I don't enjoy having someone next to me chewing popcorn, but maybe you do."

"I want to invite her home."

"To your home? Remember you don't live there now."

"To this home."

"Here? You want to bring a girl here, when you know perfectly well how impossible it is for me to talk to strangers?"

"You don't need to talk to her, she'll come to look at the books."

"Reading is a solitary act, Nephew, she will only distract you."

"You spoke of reading in the shape of a river. She improved the book I had read."

"That could be dangerous."

"The books began to seek me out when Catalina and I read the same book. You said that my emotions had opened up, and because of that the books can read me in a different way."

"I've said stupid things, false things, and useless things. One can't be wise twenty-four hours a day."

"You also said that the prince makes the rules."

"But we never spoke about a princess."

"Things change."

"If you're so set on this, why are you asking me for permission?"

"Because it's your house and I'm your nephew. I need you to be on my side. I can't find *The Wild Book* if you're not."

"Do you need me a lot a lot or just a little bit?"

"Like a nephew needs his favorite uncle."

"That's not bad at all. Do you think she likes fish? I can make something else: a floating treasure island, a thousand and one nights' cake, crepes flambéed in Dante's inferno . . . "

I left uncle going over the many books he could turn into recipes.

That afternoon I returned to the section "How to Exit the Labyrinth." I looked over the volumes about lost men. For a moment, I feared that *A Clock of Letters* might have disappeared from the shelf, but happily it was right where I'd left it.

I brought it back to my room, lay down in bed, and spent the afternoon reading about labyrinths of time. I learned that all time periods can become connected in our imaginations.

Somewhere in the labyrinth of time was *The Wild Book*, which still didn't have a reader. I was pondering the mysteries of this elusive book when Uncle told me to come down to dinner.

We ate a marine banquet: octopus soup in the style of Captain Nemo, fish à la Moby Dick, and for dessert, Billy Budd's sea-foam meringue.

Everything was delicious and was served with a side of fun anecdotes. "Dishes taste better paired with conversation than they do when paired with silence," the author of the meal explained.

At the end of the night, Uncle smiled—he had discovered how to cook stories.

Catalina in the Library

I couldn't sleep from how excited I was about inviting Catalina over to my uncle's house. Not to mention a steady bombardment of questions I asked myself: Would her mother let her come? Had she read *A Friend on the Heart-Shaped River*?

I went into the pharmacy as soon as they lifted the metal entrance gate the next morning. I was surprised to see Catalina already inside.

"There's a back door for exclusive use by employees," she explained. "We always arrive half an hour before customers do." She was chewing on an anise drop and her words smelled delicious.

Her cheeks had recovered the pale pink color I liked so much and her hair looked even more lush. Before meeting her, I didn't care how someone might chew a ragged fingernail or how they might scratch their head. But if Catalina bit her nails or scratched her head, I was captivated. I loved just watching her. If Catalina were a movie, I would live inside the cinema.

I asked her if she had read the book.

"I loved it!" was her marvelous reply. "After the other book, I thought I'd never again read anything I even just liked."

We talked about the adventure with Bruno, the singing boy lost in the forest. This time she read the exact same book I had. Perhaps because she was so tired, she didn't add any details to the story, as had happened on other occasions. In any event, this was her favorite episode.

For some reason, I felt proud, as if I were its author. Perhaps I read the book with more emotion than on other occasions, and that's why she hadn't needed to improve it.

This explanation is a bit vain, I know, but I decided to write this book with complete sincerity. Seeing Catalina's smile, I felt unusually confident. At that moment, I'd even have agreed to adopt an entire family of platypuses. Everything seemed possible.

This newfound confidence helped me when her mother approached us. Normally, I got nervous around her. Now, I calmly told her, "Catalina got sick from one book and was cured by another."

"My daughter is healthy because she takes vitamins from this pharmacy."

"The book she read yesterday helped her feel better," I insisted.

"It helped her feel cheerful, I won't deny that."

The woman looked at me with the honey-colored eyes that Catalina had inherited. Despite mistrusting the books that kept her daughter up late at night, she had given Catalina the book I'd left with her. She could have hidden it, but she didn't do that. To a certain degree, she was on our side, although she wanted to teach us a lesson. "You must control your strength," she added. "You're too young. Sooner or later, those who go to extremes wind up in this pharmacy."

"We're not extreme, Mama," Catalina protested.

"Do you think it's normal to be reading all the time? I understand that you like to do it, but even something good, when it has no limits, can become a vice."

"I feel fine. It was just one book I didn't like."

"My uncle has too many books in his library, but the most important one of all is lost and he can't find it. He wants Catalina and me to help him look for it." I looked at the woman to calculate the effect my words were having. Her face was tight, as if she hadn't yet decided on what emotion to feel.

"We're not going to read, we're going to go look for a book," Catalina explained. "The exercise will be good for me."

"It's not a question of reading strange things but of looking for a lost book," I insisted.

"What kind of book?" her mother asked.

How could I describe something I didn't know? That was like explaining what happens inside a volcano or in the depths of the ocean, where fish are blind. I dared to say, "A very . . . useful book. A book . . . "

"It's a relieving book, like the one I've just read," Catalina interrupted. "A healing book. A pharmacy book!"

The woman gave us a strange look. I would've given anything to know what was going through her mind. Catalina, who knew her much better, asked, "What's the matter with you, Mama?"

"I remembered something."

"What is it?"

"Something that happened many years ago, before you were born, when your father and I opened this pharmacy."

"What happened?"

"Your father said something very similar to what you just said. He showed me the Vademecum."

"What's that?" I asked.

"It's the book where the names of all medicines can be found, and which describes what each remedy is for," Catalina explained to me.

Her mother's eyes were locked on the wall, as if she were watching a film of her life projected on it. "Your father said, 'This is a book that cures . . . a book pharmacy: we're going to live inside this book.'" She turned to look at her daughter. "You were born and grew up in this pharmacy."

Just then I remembered what I had read in *A Clock of Letters*: sometimes time periods cross and you relive something that happened long ago.

"Alright," her mother said, "go with Juan, but be back by seven tonight. You'll feed her, won't you?" her mother asked me.

"Of course; my uncle is a great chef."

"I didn't know that."

"It's a new pastime."

"That's why he ordered so many things." She pointed to the other side of the street, where various workmen were unloading boxes with vegetables, meats, and bottles. Uncle Tito was in the doorway, looking more disheveled than ever.

"I'll be back by seven," Catalina said, and took my hand to cross the street.

"You're just like your father," the woman called at our retreating backs.

I felt an enormous happiness, as if Catalina and I were floating and nothing bad could reach us. We went to the house where Uncle was receiving all kinds of ingredients for his fabulous meals, where the hallways had thousands of sleeping books, and where we had the mission of awakening the book that had never wanted to know any reader.

"It smells so yummy!" was the first thing Catalina said when the door closed behind us.

"Do you prefer sweet or salty cronopios?" Uncle asked.

"I've never tried them."

"I'm not surprised, seeing as I've just invented them."

"What are cronopios?" Catalina asked.

"A sort of cookie in the shape of a fantastic animal. Cronopio comes from Chronos, the God of Time. The salty ones bring memories from another time and taste of tears; the sugary ones inspire hope and taste of the sweetness of future times."

"Where did you get the recipe from?" I asked Uncle.

"From some stories by Julio Cortázar, the Argentine inventor."

"Can we try them?" Catalina asked.

"Come this way."

Uncle led us to the kitchen, which was in greater disarray than ever. There were flour splotches on the ceiling and walls.

"I always lose control when an experiment turns out well," Uncle said, pointing at a plate with hundreds of cookies.

"And when one doesn't work out?" Catalina asked.

"Everything winds up looking like a battlefield and I surrender to Eufrosia's sponges and rags."

"Eufrosia is the cook," I explained to Catalina.

"Was the cook," Tito protested. "Now she is a specialist in cleaning up small, medium-sized, and large crumbs. If she were to write a book about everything she picked up in this kitchen, she could title it *A Room with a Stew*."

Catalina had a look that plainly said, "This man is even crazier than I thought."

"Do you want to try my cronopios?" Uncle asked.

He held out a plate of cookies in strange shapes: some looked like enormous microbes and others like tiny dinosaurs. They were the size of a grape. I ate a few at the same time. Their taste was strange.

Uncle noticed my confusion and said, "You ate salty and sweet cronopios at the same time. You mixed the past and the future and are tasting the flavor of the present."

"It's a curious taste."

"Indeed, dear Nephew, the present has strange flavors: you can't analyze what you haven't allowed to happen. Only the past and the future have defined flavors."

I tried a salty cronopio and liked it a lot. When I finished chewing, I tried one of the sweet ones. It tasted completely different, but was also delicious. Curiously, when I had mixed the two cookies, they'd lost their individual yumminess.

Catalina, who wasn't used to talking with Uncle, looked at him with concern.

"I think we've tried enough cookies already," I said.

The time had come for us to explore the library.

I gave Catalina the little bell. We couldn't expect her to immediately orient herself in that labyrinth of books. I tied it to her with the Margarita knot I had learned in uncle's *Atlas of Knots* and recalled the phrase he'd said about it: "Once tied, not even God can undo it."

We planned to visit each section together; at every stop, she would start checking the books in one direction and I in the other.

I described the unremarkable appearance of *The Wild Book*: a white volume that looked unfinished, of an ordinary size. An extraordinary book disguised as a poorly made one.

It seemed like a good start for us to begin our search in the place where I had almost caught *The Wild Book*.

Catalina was surprised by the randomness of the section names and laughed a lot when she found one that was called "Things That Look Like Mice."

We spent a pleasant day looking at books, commenting on titles that caught our attention, and remembering stories from *Journey Along the Heart-Shaped River*. At lunch time, Uncle sent us sandwiches so he wouldn't interrupt our work. Each sandwich was held together by a toothpick with a little bit of paper attached to it.

The first two read, "Robinson Crusoe sandwich, ideal for shipwrecks: contains crab and coconut oil." The next one said, "Three Little Pigs sandwich: contains ham, pork sausage, and bacon."

We looked through all the books in the section "How to Exit the Labyrinth" without anything strange happening. No book tried to approach us.

Would the magic not happen when we were together? Had we chosen a bad method?

"We need to be patient, like *The Wild Book*," Catalina said. "It's been in the library for many years, right? Every book likes to be read, but this one hasn't found its reader yet."

"Maybe it hates readers," I said.

"It doesn't want to be read by just anyone. That's why it's patient; it prefers to wait for a worthy reader."

"In that case, I don't think it likes us. It escaped from me."

"Maybe it just doesn't know you well enough."

I liked that Catalina had such confidence in us.

She picked up the book *A Clock of Letters* and then looked at her plastic watch: it was seven at night.

"I lost track of time. I've got to go."

We ran out of the library and almost tripped over a cat (we didn't even stop to see which one).

We reached the pharmacy a bit late, but Catalina's mother was understanding.

"Is that the book you were looking for?" She pointed to the one her daughter held in her hands.

It was only then that we realized in our hurry to get back on time, Catalina had forgotten to put *A Clock of Letters* back in its place.

"Can I keep it to read tonight?" she asked me.

Obviously, I agreed. I liked to imagine Catalina traveling through the labyrinths of time.

I went back to the house and found Eufrosia in a foul mood.

"What's the matter?" I asked her.

"Your uncle is a disaster. I spent all day cleaning. What's more, he won't let me cook. He wants me to read aloud to him, but because I don't read well he gets frustrated. Then he takes the book and reads it for himself, without putting down the spoons. The result is a disgusting mess. I want to quit."

"Please don't do that. Uncle needs you. Well, we both do."

"I'll think about it," she said, her mouth a thin line from pressing her lips together so tightly.

Uncle, naturally, was in the kitchen. He was feeding the cats their dinner.

"They're addicted to cronopios!" he exclaimed.

"Salty or sweet?"

"They like them mixed. The present tastes different to cats, what with them having nine lives and all." He poured them some milk, then added, "If you have nine lives, the present tastes like an eternity to you."

It looked like Ivory, Obsidian, and Domino were quite happy to mix the cookies that tasted of memories with the cookies that tasted of hope.

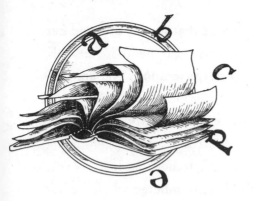

Time and Cookies

C atalina's reading of *A Clock of Letters* revealed important things to her. She took the book seemingly by accident, but once again we understood that certain stories seek out their readers. That volume with its gray cover, with an hourglass full of letters on the front, had followed her like a puppy chasing after a passerby as if hoping they'll become its owner.

The book was also of interest to her parents, she told me later. Catalina read them a few pages before going to bed, and her mother remembered the time when her daughter was younger and she used to read her stories. Now things were happening the other way around: the young girl read to her parents, who no longer had good vision (their eyes were worn out from reading the minuscule type on medications).

That night Catalina led her parents through the labyrinths of time.

Suddenly she read a sentence that greatly affected her pharmacist parents: "Books serve to remember not only what has been written, but also those things that are outside of books."

Just then, Catalina's father cried out, "My green vest!"

What had happened?

Something rather curious: her father had lost his vest in the pharmacy and suddenly remembered where he left it. He had barely uttered his exclamation when her mother shouted enthusiastically, "My silk scarf!"

She had also lost this article, and now remembered that she left it at a friend's house.

For her part, Catalina remembered where she had left the red pen she'd been looking for over the past few days, which she wanted to use when she went back to school.

How was this possible? The book provided the following explanation: "When you read something that has to do with planes, you might remember something similar: a toy plane, some object in the sky, a bird, a feathered costume, and so on."

What they read allowed them to find a vest, a scarf, and a pen.

Catalina wondered if this discovery could help us find *The Wild Book.*

The solution didn't seem easy, for the book was constantly on the move. It was like an Apache who lives in a cave, like a soldier who doesn't want to return to the army, like a fireman who flees and becomes a pyromaniac, like a Martian that doesn't adapt to Earth and wants to return to its own planet. Sometimes I felt like that, like a lonely book nobody understands and that wants to be wild so that nobody will bother it.

That night, Catalina read aloud and with great concentration, "Human beings have a personal memory in order to be able to remember things that they have experienced. Some can even remember back to their first pacifier. However, it is impossible for anyone to remember everything. Books are the external memory of mankind—a warehouse of memories."

Catalina fell silent. Could there be a book that remembered the fugitive life of *The Wild Book*?

Further on, she read something that interested her even more: "One must not forget that memories only exist in the present; someone must remember the past for it to exist, and that person is the reader. Yesterday only exists when someone remembers it *today*."

The final word appeared in italics to underscore its importance.

The next day, Catalina arrived at the library very early. She held *A Clock of Letters* up high, as if it were a firebrand, and among other fantastic things she told me, "This book helped me understand your uncle's cookies."

I looked at her closely: she was as lovely as ever, but her eyes shone even more brightly.

Just then, Catalina looked away as if she were foreseeing something.

Suddenly, there was a crunch.

The sound of footsteps came from somewhere in the house.

"Let's go to a safer place," she proposed.

"The entire house is safe," I answered. Then I thought of the Blue Book, immobilized by the Shadow Books, but I didn't say anything.

"I don't want your uncle to hear us," she said.

"Come through here," I suggested.

We went up to the statue room. Uncle never went in there.

"Who are these people?" Catalina asked.

"Famous readers of antiquity."

"I mean the photographs," she clarified, and headed to the wall where the family images were hung.

She had been more interested in the portraits than in the imposing statues.

"This is my father." I pointed to the photograph taken when he was a boy.

"He looks like your little brother." Catalina smiled.

Then she looked at me so closely it made me feel nervous. She declared seriously, "You no longer have a child's face."

She kept looking over the photographs and suddenly asked, "Who is she?"

Out of all the images she had chosen the one of my mother sleeping.

"My mom," I answered.

"She's so pretty. It looks like she's dreaming something really nice. I'd like to meet her. Where is she?"

I asked her if we could sit down on the floor, and, more calmly than I would have believed I was capable of doing so, I told her that my parents had separated. I spoke to her of the mashed potatoes that tasted of ash and of the bridges my father built. The last of which was in Paris.

I spoke softly, as if my mother might wake up in her portrait.

She asked me to keep talking about them, and I told her my father built enormous bridges and buildings with the plastic cubes I had. He was able to make everything keep its balance. His hands never trembled when he placed the final piece of a tower.

"You admire him a lot, don't you?" she asked.

Until just then, I'd never thought of that. I was angry with my father because he had left, but I also missed him and wanted to see him again. I was realizing how much I admired him, which was rather confusing.

Catalina took my hand and caressed my palm, as if she were tracing the curls of a shell. "The spirals of time," she told me. "Memories move like this, like a circle that comes back but doesn't return to its starting point unchanged."

Everything seemed to me to be strange and lovely. She held my hand and I could smell her hair, which had an aroma of chamomile or perhaps some flower that didn't exist. I saw the lobe of her ear, covered in golden fuzz like the skin of a peach, and I didn't understand any of her explanations about time—I only knew that what she spoke of was essential to our finding *The Wild Book*.

Then she stood up and walked through the room. I listened to her, feeling a little calmer now.

"This room is perfect for what I want to tell you." Her footsteps squeaked on the wooden floorboards. "It's not odd that your uncle has prepared those cookies."

"The cronopios?"

"Yes, the cronopios."

"Why?"

"Because he has only lived in the past or the future. His life has had no present. His only family has been these photographs on the wall. He has never shared anything with anyone. That's why he can't find *The Wild Book*."

"I don't understand," I said sincerely.

"I memorized a phrase from *A Clock of Letters*," she said. "It goes like this: 'Someone must remember the past for it to exist, and that person is the reader. Yesterday only exists when someone remembers it *today*.'"

She paused, opening her hands like a magician after performing a trick, and asked, "Do you see?"

I only saw that her arms were spread very wide.

"I don't understand," I said again, afraid she'd think I was an idiot.

"Your uncle reads and reads but he doesn't share his life with anyone, he doesn't do anything. He just remembers or imagines things. He has very little life."

"Can one have a lot of life or just a little?"

"He only has an imaginary life."

"But he wants to find *The Wild Book*. That's something!"

"He can't find it because he doesn't know how to act. His present is insipid, that's why his cookies only taste good if they have to do with the past or the future."

"But, what has all this got to do with us?" I asked her.

"It has to do with *The Wild Book*."

"How?"

"Books that are already written come from the past. Books that are going to be written belong to the future. *The Wild Book* is extremely rare because it is in the present: it hasn't yet been read; it is a book that's about to happen! It will write itself when it has a reader. That is what it needs, someone living, someone who feels today what happened a long time ago: a true reader."

She paused for a long moment to stare at a bearded statue and added, "Do you know what I think?"

"What?"

"That your uncle lied to us."

"About what?"

"Something tells me that he did see *The Wild Book*."

"How do you know?"

"It's just a feeling I have. He talks about the book with great familiarity, as if he has seen it. Perhaps the book felt that your uncle wasn't alive enough and therefore was mistrustful of him. Your uncle is afraid that something might happen. *The Wild Book* is like a horse that has never been ridden. It needs a special rider—someone it can trust."

Could it be possible that she was right? Had Uncle had the chance to read *The Wild Book* and either changed his mind or got rejected by those indomitable pages?

"Your uncle communicates his emotions through his dishes," added Catalina, who was on a roll. "He doesn't dare say that he was afraid of *The Wild Book*, but his cronopios gave him away. Do you know what your uncle needs?"

She paused, and in the silence I heard the quick thumping of my heart.

"To be shaken up," she said, quite naturally.

"Shaken up?"

"Yes. In the pharmacy we have some medicines that say 'Shake well before use.' See, some of it settles in the bottom of the bottle and the whole thing must be shaken in order for it to work."

"My uncle is not a medicine."

"He needs shaking to recover some intensity, to live with intention, to be daring, and to let exciting things happen." Catalina's hands moved so quickly that they seemed to be electrified. "Now is the moment for him to stop living like one of these statues and to do something."

She was so frenzied that I wondered if there was a medicine she should take with a label that read, "Calm down before use."

I didn't dare contradict her. Right then I would have followed her to a battlefield, even if my only weapon were a peashooter.

We went to the kitchen, where Tito was breading zucchinis.

"How good to see you, book explorers!"

Catalina's excitement had been contagious. I stared my uncle in the face and spoke to him with a seriousness that surprised us all. "We want to ask you a question, but you must promise to tell the truth."

"Is it about my recipes?"

"No."

"Then I don't care. My concoctions are an artistic secret. Everything else can be known, even be published in the newspapers! Ask whatever you wish! Shoot, detective."

"Did you ever touch *The Wild Book*?"

"Well, technically . . ."

"You promised you would tell us the truth."

"If you want I'll give you one of my recipes. I could sacrifice a small culinary secret. Would you like to know how one makes quince cheese?"

"What is *The Wild Book* like?"

Uncle was silent for a moment, then finally said, "It has a frayed aspect, like a woman who goes out into the street without first combing her hair. Sorry, I'm a bit nervous. It has the aspect of an unfinished book, one which hasn't yet been printed. That is its magic: it will only be completed when it finds its reader."

"And you opened it?" I asked.

"Let me take a sip of tea."

Uncle raised his cup to his lips and drank noisily. The tea slid down his chin but he didn't bother to dry it. He spoke again, more nervously than bad-humoredly: "What is this? An interrogation? What am I accused of?"

"I only want to know if you opened the book."

"Why?"

"To know if it has ever allowed someone from this house to hold it."

"It's very slippery. It escapes easily. If books were athletes, this one would be an Olympic champion."

"We already know that."

"You've never spoken to me like this, Nephew."

"Do you want to find *The Wild Book?*"

"Of course."

"Then why won't you help me?"

"I help you in every way I can. I prepare delicious meals, Eufrosia washes your clothes and folds your socks, and I let your girlfriend come to my house."

I looked toward Catalina, trying not to blush. She was lovely and calm. My voice trembled as I said, "Catalina is not my girlfriend."

I regretted saying it immediately. Would she interpret it as a rejection? I couldn't keep track of so many different thoughts at the same time.

Uncle continued, "Well, I let your lovely young friend, who I wish were your girlfriend, come to my house."

"Do you want to find *The Wild Book* or not?" I asked, furious.

"Calm down," Catalina said, and took my hand.

Then she turned to my uncle. "We want to help you."

Uncle made a face I'd never seen before. He looked like he was about to cry. Without realizing it, I'd made him emotional. His eyes were sad but at the same time full of affection. He looked at me as if I were pulling away from him on a ship, leaving him behind, alone, on the pier.

I looked at Catalina. She, too, seemed very full of emotion.

"What's happening to you, Uncle?" I asked at last.

"A few weeks ago, when you arrived, I felt like I would finally manage to find *The Wild Book*. Since you were little you've had the powers of a great reader. I was very pleased to confirm that the years hadn't turned you into a senseless brute and that you still attracted books. Then, when you opened your heart to this young woman, who regrettably is not your girlfriend, I knew that you were not just a special reader; you are a super-special reader. I was enormously pleased to know that after so many years of trying, someone could finally find the book that nobody had been able to read. But then something strange happened."

"What?"

"It's difficult to say, Nephew."

"Say what you must."

"I'll just spit it out, without even taking a sip of tea to make it more palatable."

Uncle placed a large and heavy hand on my head. "I don't know if I want you to find the book," he said, in a very deep voice.

"Why? Could something bad happen?"

"Something bad could happen to me."

"What?"

"If you find the book, the adventure will have finished."

"And?"

"That means that being here will no longer be important to you. That means you'll go somewhere else and I'll stop seeing you."

Uncle looked at me, and for the first time his eyes didn't seem so protuberant. Suddenly, his face looked like that of an old and gentle sage. He turned to me and spoke words that I never thought I would hear him say. "I love you, Nephew." He looked at Catalina and said, "And you too, even though I only know you a little. I don't want to wind up alone."

Catalina brought her mouth to my ear. Her words brushed my ear like a quick breeze. "I think he's shaken up enough," she whispered.

I looked at my uncle and I told him, "You don't need to be alone. I can visit you or you can come to my mother's house."

"Go out into the city, where people stink and always talk about money, where dogs do their business on the sidewalk and the cars move too fast?"

"You could invite us for lunch once a week."

"Promise me that if you find *The Wild Book* you won't stop visiting me?"

"I promise you."

"What did you want to know?" he asked and crossed his arms, as if we had only now begun to talk.

I was so moved by what my uncle had said that I'd also forgotten what Catalina and I had wanted to find out. "I don't know," I muttered.

Fortunately, Catalina hadn't lost the thread of the conversation. "We would like to know if you ever opened *The Wild Book*."

"Yes. I opened it just once. It was my great chance, and I wasted it."

Catalina asked, "What happened?"

"I felt horribly afraid."

"Why?" I asked. "Is it a horror book?"

"It is something even more powerful."

"What?" Catalina and I asked in unison.

"It is a mirror." Uncle swallowed. "I felt that I was looking at my reflection. I told you before that books are mirrors, but this one is different: it is for brave people who are willing to immerse themselves in a book, to be sucked through it, to feel so attuned to its emotions that it's almost as if they were writing the book themselves."

"Did you read a little from the book?" Catalina asked.

"I didn't manage to read it. I saw just whiteness and

yet I felt that the book was portraying me. I was afraid of recognizing myself, of immersing myself in its pages and coming to terms with who I am. I closed the book right away."

"And what happened?" Catalina asked.

"The book disappeared. I wasn't worthy to be its reader. I never saw it again."

Catalina had been right. Uncle was afraid that something too intense would happen to him.

"What section did you find it in?"

"I remember the bookcase where I encountered the book: 'Motors That Make No Noise.' You already know I detest loud sounds. I wanted to see if I might find a silent blender for Eufrosia's vegetable chopping. And there it was! *The Wild Book*! Later I understood why I found it there: a book is an apparatus, a mechanism, a motor that functions and makes no noise."

"Do you think it might have returned there?" Catalina asked.

"It's very possible. Books are insistent. That's why they become classics."

"Have you ever gone to that section?" Catalina asked me.

"Once."

"And what happened?"

"I like cars but motors don't interest me very much: I browsed through it quickly."

"You didn't see anything odd? Try to remember."

"Shall I bring you a salty cronopio?" Uncle suggested.

"Wait a minute!" I exclaimed.

"What happened?" Uncle's eyes were bulging once more.

"Something strange did happen! There were books about horsepower in the motors section."

"That's logical, Nephew. But I suppose that's not what you want to tell us."

"No. When I was already leaving, a book fell to the floor. I picked it up and put it back on its shelf."

"And?" Uncle came so close to me that I could smell the smudge of tomato sauce on his cheek.

Then I recited, as if I were talking in my sleep, "It was called *Horsepower without Horseshoes*."

"That's obvious, Nephew, what else did you expect? Engines don't have hooves."

"But horses without horseshoes are wild ones," I said. Nobody has ridden them; they haven't been tamed."

"Like *The Wild Book*!" Uncle said. "The book was giving you a sign."

"Now I get it," I said, very surprised.

Catalina said aloud what was running through everyone's mind. "Let's go there."

Motors that Make no Noise

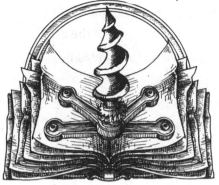

When we entered the section "Motors That Make No Noise," Catalina went to the back of the room and I stayed near the door. We decided to examine the area book by book, title by title, author by author, until we found our prey.

About twenty minutes had passed when suddenly something began to buzz. It seemed to be the rumbling of pipes or perhaps of some other apparatus elsewhere in the house. At first I thought Uncle was using the blender, but the buzzing went on for too long for that to be likely.

I looked at the shelf in front of me; incredibly, it seemed to be vibrating, as if a subway were traveling beneath the house. But there was no subway in this part of the city.

Catalina's eyes shone from the back of the room. Her expression was that of someone observing something very interesting that might turn dangerous. With hand gestures, she asked me to come closer.

I took a few steps and something curious happened. It wasn't really a sound—it was something else; it was as if the air were becoming more concentrated, as if the silence were suddenly audible, as if the room's energy were about to implode.

Catalina showed me the book she had not let go of since she had arrived at the house: *A Clock of Letters.*

She placed her index finger to her lips so I wouldn't say anything. Then she showed me the book she had found: *Adjustments in Time.* I thought this was a book that had been shelved in the wrong section, but when I opened it I realized that it was about mechanics. It was a manual on how to adjust motors to their appropriate rhythms. I didn't know that a motor could be out of step with time.

Catalina asked me to put the book back on its shelf and placed *A Clock of Letters* next to it. The buzzing stopped immediately. She smiled in a marvelous way.

Then she signaled that we should leave the room.

"What was that all about?" I asked her.

"That was a good sign. The books became restless when we arrived. Did you notice the buzzing?"

"Of course."

"They sounded like motors about to jump-start. It was as if we were the fuel they needed."

Catalina seemed to understand the mysteries of the library better than I did.

Although many years have passed since then, I still remember that she wore a blue blouse with yellow stars embroidered at the neck. I'll never forget a single detail from that moment when I asked her, burning with curiosity, "And why did you leave *A Clock of Letters* there?"

"We had to send them a sign. Books mingle among themselves, your uncle told us that. Now these two books are together: one is about human time and the other is about motor time. We'll see what takes place."

"What do you think will happen?"

"*The Wild Book* has been very calm. Do you remember the blue trout in the Heart-Shaped River?"

How could I forget it? That was one of my favorite adventures. Ernesto and Marina get into a canoe to fish. They spend all afternoon catching fish. Before returning to camp, they looked at what they'd caught: lots of fish but nothing special. All the fish were very small and wouldn't make a decent meal. Then they realized that those fish could be tasty, not to them, but to a fish from the depths. They hadn't caught their own meal, but that of the fish they wanted to catch! Right away, they placed the small fish on the hooks and sunk the sinkers very low. After various attempts, they caught a blue trout, a very rare species notable for its large size. Its flesh was prized for its taste and the witches of the region attributed great magical powers to its scales.

Sometimes you catch something that seems insignificant, but that can be used to catch something else. The good fisherman catches easy fish that help him reel in what is truly worthwhile. It's similar with people: you need to meet enough of them to find the ones who truly interest you.

"*The Wild Book* is like the blue trout," Catalina explained.

"You put *A Clock of Letters* there as bait?"

"Yes. It's a book it can identify with."

"And why did you want us to leave the room? It would be thrilling to see how the books move."

"It would be fabulous, but your uncle says that the books don't like for us to see them moving. Soon you'll find one without knowing how it got there."

"Of course: if they moved openly, people would be afraid of them or would use them for target practice. They'd hunt them like wild animals. Humans are capable of anything."

Catalina stared at me for a while and said, "And what do you like?"

I didn't answer and she insisted, "What is your blue trout?"

What did she mean? What bait could interest me?

"*The Wild Book*, I guess," I answered.

"And nothing else?" she asked without taking her eyes off mine.

I'm sure I blushed. I wanted to find *The Wild Book*, but above all I wanted to be with Catalina, and I was embarrassed to tell her so. She seemed to be waiting for me to say something important. I didn't want to make a mistake and disappoint her.

"You're trembling." Catalina placed her hand on my cheek. "Like a book about to be read!" She smiled.

She had realized that I was in love with her. She read me like a book, but I was a book muted with embarrassment.

It was a relief when Catalina said, "Let's go see what happened."

We went into the room again, which was still utterly silent. We walked slowly toward the shelf where she had left *A Clock of Letters*.

When we got there, everything looked like it had before. We saw no signs of a white book.

But we also didn't find *A Clock of Letters*.

We looked at one another in silence, and suddenly a little girl's voice shouted, "Juanito!"

It was Carmen. She was here at last. Eufrosia followed behind her, carrying a heavy suitcase. My sister's hands were full of her stuffed animals, among them her toy named Juanito.

"Is she your girlfriend?" Carmen asked me.

I didn't answer. Instead I looked at the three cats that had followed my sister.

Catalina didn't reply either; she just smiled and looked calmly at Carmen, as if the question didn't bother her.

My face had turned as red as a tomato, and my sister said, "Oops, I said something I shouldn't have! Uncle Tito told me that you have a girlfriend who you're madly in love with, but that you don't like it when people say she's your girlfriend."

"This is Catalina."

"Hello," Catalina said with an admirably cheerful tone.

"Is the Shadow Club here?" Carmen asked.

"What is the Shadow Club?" Catalina wanted to know.

"A place one can only go at night," I answered.

"And is it in this house?" my sister insisted.

I remembered the room of books for the blind and said, "Yes."

"Woo-hoo!" Carmen was happy. "Will you take me?"

"Of course," I answered, even if I wasn't completely sure I'd be able to keep my promise.

"Shall I introduce you to my new stuffed animals?" Carmen lined up her toys on the shelf, knocking some books to the floor.

Uncle walked in just then. He was armed with a magnifying glass. "Not a single stuffed animal is to move! I need to inspect them all to make sure they're clean."

"I washed them last week," Carmen informed us.

"That's not enough. I need to examine them one by one. Catalina?"

"Yes?"

"I know you have experience with the sick. I ask for your aid in helping me to examine these patients."

"They are not patients," Carmen cried. "They're my animals!"

"For now, my dear niece, they are patients suspected of having fungi under their ears and in other hard-to-wash places. Let's get to it."

Uncle asked Eufrosia to place the stuffed animals in a row. He pulled another magnifying glass from his pocket and gave it to Catalina. They examined ears, eyes, paws, claws, jaws, and noses without finding anything.

Uncle Tito was satisfied with the inspection. "These stuffed animals are as healthy as an apple," he declared contentedly.

Carmen introduced me to the ones I didn't know. She showed me a rabbit that had terrible tummy aches, a hare that was always nervous, and a turtle prone to headaches, just like our mother.

"Here they're going to be much calmer and they'll be cured of everything," I told Carmen.

She gave me a hug and I noticed that she'd grown a little in the weeks since we had last seen one another.

I helped gather up the stuffed animals and was astonished by Eufrosia's ability to pick up seven of them in one hand.

I looked at Catalina and a chill ran down my back.

Her eyes, already large to begin with, were open so wide they looked enormous.

She was looking at something behind me. Something important. Something that made her glow with excitement.

I turned around. What I saw made me wish I had the harpoon of Captain Ahab, the sailor who battled against Moby Dick. Catalina's attention hadn't been caught by the sudden appearance of a whale, but in the upper region of one bookcase I saw the thing that held her transfixed:

the white spine of a book that hadn't been there a few moments before. It was a softcover book; a book disguised as an ordinary volume without any visible letters, as if it had still not finished being made. It was the book that had never been read.

I hurried toward the bookcase. Uncle saw what I was doing and let out a high cry, Eufrosia let all the stuffed animals fall, Carmen stumbled, and I tripped over her. By the time I had finally managed to reach the right spot, it was no longer the right spot.

The Wild Book had disappeared again.

That night it was very hard for me to fall asleep. I heard noises in the room next to mine, where my sister now slept. Around midnight she came in to ask me to take her to the Shadow Club.

I told her I couldn't, not that night.

Then she wanted to sleep in my bed. I didn't like for her to sleep with me because she liked to dream that she was flying and would spread her arms wide, taking up the whole bed. I couldn't sleep like that. Besides, I was already too grown-up to share my bed with children.

"Let's go to your room. I'll stay with you until you fall asleep," I told her.

"I'm not tired," was her reply.

She always said that. I took her back to her room and five minutes later she was fast asleep.

I returned to my room, more fully awake than ever. I envied the speed with which Carmen could fall asleep and adapt herself to anything.

I was thinking and thinking about *The Wild Book*.

Would we have another chance to catch it? We'd failed this time, but had been so close.

I lay motionless, listening to the crackling of the house until I felt that the sounds had become the crackling of my own ideas.

The last time I checked the clock before falling asleep, it was three in the morning.

Once more I dreamed of the scarlet room, but this time something different happened. I heard the lament that emerged from the end of the hallway and I walked toward it with my heavy iron boots. I entered the room with the red walls, but there wasn't blood on them, it was just a room painted red. I had always liked that color and being there didn't bother me. I heard the complaining noise again coming from a corner of the room. It seemed like a woman's cry. I walked toward it and saw something wrapped in a cloth. It was a small bundle, but I couldn't lift it. It weighed more than my iron boots. I tried to pull it from under the cloth and I couldn't do that either. It was a wrapping without knots or openings. Something inside it was crying.

I knelt down and ran my hands over the bundle carefully. It seemed to me that it was a book. Curiously, once

I recognized its shape it became lighter and I was able to pick it up.

What could one do with a book that cried? Was there a way to comfort it?

I looked around the room and discovered a door I hadn't noticed before. It had three locks. Luckily, each lock had a key in it. I opened the door and was dazzled by a shining brilliance. It was nighttime in the room, but beyond the door it was day, radiant with light.

The scarlet room led onto a field illuminated by a brilliant midday sun. The sunlight penetrated even through the bundle wrapped in the cloth, and the book inside stopped crying.

I walked out onto the field and felt the grass beneath my feet. I no longer wore iron boots. The cloth, which until then had been of an imprecise color, became a red-and-white checked fabric, like a tablecloth. I tried to open it, but I couldn't do so this time either.

I walked up a hill and sat down to look at the landscape. I remembered the photo of my mother sleeping and I lay down on the grass. I fell deeply asleep. I slept within my dream. At one moment, I worried that I couldn't wake but then I thought, "Yes, I can, because I am in my dream and I decide what happens." I opened my eyes and it was as if I woke up twice, once in my dream and once outside of it.

I was in my bed, in Uncle Tito's house.

I tried to go back to sleep, to return to the field and find out what happened with that mysterious book, but it is much easier to flee from a dream than to return to it.

In any event, I felt calmer than I ever had before. For the first time, I had managed to leave the scarlet room. More importantly, I had managed to save a book, a book that cried like a child.

Perhaps what the book wanted was to be adopted; perhaps in passing from the scarlet room to the field it had ceased to be a child and had grown up.

If I ever had that dream again, I thought, I would carry scissors to cut the cloth and find out what book it was covering.

I never got to carry out my plan because I never again had the nightmare about the scarlet room.

I had lost my fear of what happened there. Instead, my curiosity to know what a book that had never been read might contain had grown.

A Zigzag
Radiation

I thought my sister would be bored at Uncle's house, but the opposite happened. She loved to carry her stuffed animals into the kitchen. She would tie a napkin around the neck of each one and spend long hours keeping Uncle company.

He needed someone to read aloud to him stories that would inspire recipes, and Carmen turned into his assistant. Thanks to this teamwork, we enjoyed the exquisite dish "Late Rabbit" which occurred to him after hearing Carmen read *Alice in Wonderland*.

While Uncle and Carmen turned stories into meals, Catalina and I went through the books in the section "Motors That Make No Noise." But there were no further advances after our initial success.

Then, Catalina said something I never expected her to say.

"I miss the pharmacy."

It was a normal thing to say. After all, that was where she worked during her vacations and where her parents were. However, it could also mean something horrible: was she giving up the search?

I proposed that we take a break from looking for *The Wild Book* and instead search for a new adventure on the Heart-Shaped River.

She agreed, but it wasn't easy for us to find one of these stories that could turn up anywhere in the house.

We were very tired by dinnertime. The rich smell of the food comforted us a little, and I asked Uncle, "Why do the stories about the Heart-Shaped River never appear in the same place in the library?"

"It's a book that likes to catch its readers by surprise. It's a hunter of a book."

"And *The Wild Book* is a book that doesn't want to be hunted," Catalina added.

"That's right," Uncle said. "Books like to be found in a way that is similar to the story written in their pages. The adventures of the Heart-Shaped River take place in a forest where one needs to fish and hunt; that's why it also wants its readers to find its episodes as if the library they were searching through were a wild forest. One must remember that books are made from trees, so this library could be considered a forest after all."

"If we knew what *The Wild Book* was about, we could approach it in a way that was similar to its story," I said.

"Of course we could, Nephew, but we don't know what it's about."

The next day I feared Catalina wouldn't come to the house. I was ecstatic when I heard the doorbell ring. She had arrived filled with enthusiasm and ready to find another episode of the Heart-Shaped River. She gave me an anise drop to sweeten my journey along the hallways that crisscrossed Uncle's house.

We decided to split up to improve our chances. I wanted to give the bell to Catalina, but Carmen had tied it to a stuffed bunny that, according to her, got easily upset. "If I take it off, she gets sad," she told me.

This put me in a foul mood. My sister was too childish. If we kept paying attention to her silly caprices, we'd never get anywhere. This was not a toy store. It was a library where a fantastic book was hidden.

In order to calm me down, Uncle came up with an emergency remedy: he gave Catalina a tambourine so that she could summon us in case she got lost. It was a bit absurd to wander through the library with a tambourine in one hand, but it was an effective remedy.

In the adventures of the river I had learned that during an emergency, one needed to not fixate on the details—if a sock could serve as a tourniquet to stop a hemorrhage, one shouldn't complain that it was a smelly sock.

It must have been around two in the afternoon when I heard the jingling of the tambourine.

The sound came from upstairs.

It's very strange how things happen. When Catalina and I split up, it seemed fine to me that she would wander around the entire house. But when I heard the tambourine and approached the place where the sound came from, I began to feel strangely uneasy that she was in that area of the library.

I walked down the hallway that led, of all places, to the room where I had locked up the evil Blue Book. Luckily, Catalina wasn't inside. She was waiting for me in the hallway.

"Guess what?" she asked.

"What?"

"I found what we're looking for right here, on the floor." Catalina pointed to the rug, which was strewn with various books. They were the same ones I had knocked over when I'd hid in the hallway! However, at the time I hadn't noticed that our so-interesting adventure was among these piles of texts.

I remembered perfectly that scene that had taken place in the depths of the night: Uncle had walked by me, grumbling about Eufrosia and the disordered state of the house, complaining that nobody had put the books back in their place. Curiously, one of these books was the one we were looking for: it was titled *Midnight on the Heart-Shaped River*.

I proposed to Catalina that we go read it in the fern room, which I liked so much. She sat beside me on the puffy sofa, and for the first time we read a book at the same time.

"Ready?" she asked me whenever she finished a page, to make sure I was still with her.

In this episode, everything in the story took place at night. It was about a strange radioactive material that was buried in a hill by some thieves. A group of forest rangers came to search the area and asked for help from Eagle Eye and from Ernesto and Marina, who had become famous for their way of taking care of the forest.

The rangers explained that the radioactive material had disappeared from a nuclear reactor that produced electricity. It was very valuable and the thieves had asked for a ransom for it. Clues they'd discovered indicated that it was hidden in the forest. The only way to find it was to use special glasses to detect the green light emitted by the radioactive material, which was protected by a metal box. However, its light was so powerful that it managed to pierce the metal case at night. Even if it were underground, it would send zigzagging signals up to the surface, producing an electric green light that would last mere seconds, but that could be detected by alert and watchful eyes.

The forest was enormous. They needed the eyes of many people concentrating solely on this task if they hoped to find the metal box. Eagle Eye could spot a baby owl fifty meters away in the darkest part of the forest, but finding the radioactive material was going to prove to be even more difficult than that.

The terrible thing about the whole matter was that if the material wasn't found in time, it could contaminate this natural reserve. The radiation would affect all the wildlife—strange creatures would be born: quails with three legs, blue bears, and blind eagles.

We read the story in a rush and soon reached the moment when Marina and Ernesto were exploring the forest at midnight. Suddenly, they saw a greenish reflection.

Just then, the lines of the book seemed to start vibrating. I thought perhaps my eyes were just tired from so much reading. I rubbed my eyelids hard. When I looked at the book again, Ernesto and Marina were moving over the dry leaves toward a green, shimmering light. They had found the radioactive material that was threatening to poison the forest.

I looked at Catalina—she had her eyes closed.

"What's the matter?" I asked her.

"I thought the letters moved. Then I saw a too-bright light."

I was looking at a green glow—could we be seeing the same thing?

"What color?" I asked her.

"Green," she replied.

Behind the glow, the letters seemed to move from left to right, as if they were being printed on the page as we read. I couldn't see what they said because the light was too intense.

Seconds later, the book recovered its normal appearance.

"I saw the glow, too. The book lit up."

"That's the same thing I saw." Catalina laid her head against my chest and put my arm over her shoulder.

We continued reading.

Ernesto and Marina found the metal case, buried deep beneath the earth (its radiation was so powerful that the beams moved up through the earth in thin, zigzagging rays).

They ran to find Eagle Eye, who used his famous coyote howls to summon the forest rangers.

In the last part of the book, a team of specialists armed with special suits and gloves dug up the contaminating material. The box was treated with the utmost caution. Cords were tied around it and then attached to a helicopter. The case was then transferred back to the electricity plant.

We liked the story a lot but were left wondering why the letters had moved and shimmered. What had we just experienced? The book had shone as if it truly contained something radioactive in its pages.

We opened the book again to page 198. We didn't find anything strange or suspicious. The letters were arranged as unremarkably as the smooth surface of a quiet pond. But we knew that this surface could become quite choppy.

Night fell in the fern room. Through the skylight we saw the moon, shaped like a slice of watermelon.

Catalina gave me another anise drop and we spent a while in silence, happy to be together and enjoying one another's company without needing to say anything more.

We were both thinking about the strange effect the book had had on us, but we didn't need to say anything.

When the anise drops had dissolved in our mouths, we went to see Uncle.

We found him coated in flour up to his eyebrows, standing beside a fan that was turned off.

"This is the absolute worst moment," he told us. "Can you believe this?" He pointed at my sister and her animals, all covered in flour.

"What happened?" I asked him.

"I turned on this fan and look what happened."

I looked up: hundreds of cherries had somehow ended up stuck on the ceiling.

"Who said that cooking is soothing?" he asked irritably.

The situation was lots of fun for Carmen, because it gave her the chance to fill the washtub with warm water and give all her animals another bath.

Uncle wiped his face with his usual clumsiness; he forgot to rub his eyebrows, which remained whitened with flour. He only realized his carelessness when an ant climbed up there in search of sustenance.

"I'm going to bathe my eyebrows and I'll be with you in a second," Uncle said.

When he was finally ready, he approached us with his usual cup of tea and listened to what we had to tell him.

He listened with great attention to the story of the book that had lit up.

When we were finished, he didn't say anything for a long time. Then he said, "You have gotten a taste of the force of reading. Words transmit energy—that's why you saw them shine. By reading together, the two of you duplicated their intensity. I'm surprised the pages didn't wind up catching fire."

"The page shone when the characters found the radioactive material," I clarified.

"Of course," Uncle replied. "You were excited and wanted to see it. When you read you never see the letters; you see the things the letters are about, like a forest, a house turned into a library, or a pharmacy. Books serve as mirrors and windows—they're full of images."

Just then, Catalina looked at the clock.

"It's time for me to go," Catalina said.

"Before you go, dear, I must tell you something," Uncle informed us.

"What about?" I asked.

"What is happening to you is very important. The book wanted to tell you something more."

"Something more?" Catalina asked.

"The greatest stories make you think of your own stories. *Midnight on the Heart-Shaped River* is about a dangerous substance buried in the forest. Something the forest must be freed from. A book is like a pond: it shows one story on the surface and another in its depths. Doesn't it occur to you that there might be something beneath what you read?"

"Beneath?"

"A story hidden beneath that story—a similar story but one that has to do with the two of you. Is there something you must get rid of in the night? Something similar to that radiation that almost destroyed the forest?"

I remembered the dream of the scarlet room in which I took the book out onto the field. I saved the book from its sadness, but I also saved myself from the crying book.

"It's possible that there is something," I said.

"What is it?" Uncle asked.

"I can't tell you," I replied.

I thought about the Blue Book. It was still in the house. I had to get it out of there. It was our radioactive material. Although we couldn't see it, other books could feel that something evil emerged from there, like the green, zigzagging light. While that harmful book was among us, *The Wild Book* would remain mistrustful.

Catalina and Uncle stared at me but I didn't tell them anything about the book with the blue cover. I didn't want anyone else to have to deal with it. I don't know why I acted this way. I guess there are moments when one feels the need to do things for others without their knowing it.

I had to finish what I started. The enemy could not live among us. Even if it were controlled by the Shadow Books, it was necessary to get it out of here.

"What's happening to you?" Uncle asked, very surprised by my silence.

I'm sure my face betrayed my bold thoughts.

"There's something I need to take care of alone."

Catalina looked at me, puzzled. "Can't we help you?"

"For us to remain together, I've got to take care of something," I said, with newfound confidence.

"You have to 'take care of something,' Nephew? Can't you be more specific?"

"No."

That "something" had a blue cover.

The Shadow Club

That night I didn't put my pajamas on. I spent a long time in my room until I couldn't hear anything but the squeaks and groans that old houses make, as if they were remembering the footsteps of all the people who had ever walked down their hallways.

I had to act alone. Uncle couldn't come into contact with the evil book again, for he had shown himself to be weaker than me. I also didn't want to put Catalina at risk.

In the stories of the Heart-Shaped River, Ernesto and Marina were usually faced with the decision of what path to take in the middle of the forest. When there were two possibilities, each of them took a different route to confront their own dangers. If one of them encountered something terrible, the other might rescue them.

The time had come for me to do something similar. If the Blue Book hurt me or drove me crazy, the others could continue the search for *The Wild Book*.

I opened the door, ready to act in total solitude, but I found Carmen sitting in the hallway.

"I've been waiting for you," she said.

She carried her Juanito under one arm.

"Are you going to the Shadow Club?" she asked me.

Could I lie to her? My sister looked at me with enormous trust.

"Your animals need you to take care of them tonight," I told her, trying to buy myself enough time to think of a good excuse.

"They've just elected a president. Campanito the rabbit was chosen, and he told me that I could go with you."

Carmen lived in a fantasy world that enabled her every desire.

I had no argument to prevent her from coming with me, so I ended up replying with what I least thought I'd find myself saying that night: "OK, you can come with me."

I picked up the flashlight I had brought from our house (I knew that I wasn't going camping, but it made me feel good to pack it), and I walked over the wooden floor that creaked on every third step. My sister took my hand and with her other held Juanito.

Carmen marveled at how well I knew every nook and cranny of that big house full of twisted hallways, uneven steps, and bookcases that blocked our way.

We walked toward the part of the library where the air smelled as if it had been interred for years. Then we reached the rooms where it seemed as though there was more dust than there was air. At the hallway where the wooden floor was the creakiest, we noticed a strange scent of excitement and fear. It smelled like a creature from a bygone time. It smelled like a dragon.

We stopped in front of the room of the Shadow Books. An owl hooted outside in the darkness, and a clock ticktocked somewhere in the house.

Were there owls around here? Could it be an imaginary owl? Did the clock make that hooting noise? I had too many questions.

To calm myself down a little, I told Carmen that our great-grandfather and our great-uncle had both been blind. I talked to her about the Shadow Books and about the Blue Book.

"The good books are guarding it," I added.

"Is it a bespelled book?" she asked.

"It is an evil book."

"Are you going to destroy it?"

It was a good question and one I hadn't considered. I only knew that I had an outstanding matter to deal with waiting in that room: I had left a book in there that should not be in the library. It wasn't good to have such a dangerous prisoner.

"Are you going to burn it?" Carmen insisted.

Then I remembered a passage from *Midnight on the Heart-Shaped River*. Ernesto asked the forest rangers if the radioactive material could be destroyed to keep it from causing problems. They told him, "That would cause even greater damage: it could contaminate the entire forest." Then Eagle Eye said, "If you find a tree that has a plague, the worst thing you can do is burn it. By trying to save yourself from that one tree, you could provoke a blaze and destroy all the others." Marina concluded the discussion: "Trees are like books: if you dare try to burn one, you run the risk of burning them all."

One could not destroy a book, no matter how evil it was. Even if it were a Pirate Book that robs and destroys the words of others.

The adventures of the Heart-Shaped River were giving me clues to what I needed to do in my own life. "I must not destroy that harmful book, but I must get it out of the house, like I did in the dream of the scarlet room," I thought. Yes, that was the solution.

Feeling confident in my plan, I opened the door to the room. I was so nervous that I forgot to turn off the flashlight. The Shadow Books didn't like that at all. Two or three of them, rather heavy ones, fell on my neck. The flashlight fell to the floor and turned off. I heard a slam behind me. There was no further movement.

"Juan?" my sister called.

I tried to see her but the darkness was very thick. I walked toward her and tripped over the books that had fallen to the floor.

Finally, I touched something fuzzy. I thought it was Juanito, but it had long ears.

"I also brought Andrés," Carmen explained. "He was hidden in my nightgown. Foxes are very clever, and Andrés is the most cunning fox of all."

Carmen gave me her hand in the darkness.

We hadn't felt so alone since our father had left home.

"What are we doing?" she asked.

I didn't have the least idea of what we should do, but I was certain of one thing: we couldn't be afraid. I was filled with a strange sense of foreboding in that room. I felt that everything hinged on this moment. If we managed to do something as important as freeing ourselves from the malignant book, we would prove to have lots of strength. A strength that would stay with us forever—even if Papa went far away and Mama smoked and worried about everything.

"I'll take care of you," I told Carmen.

"And later you'll take me to Paris?"

"Yes."

"We'll see the bridge Papa is building?"

"Yes."

"And then we'll go back to Mama?"

"Yes."

"And you'll drive the car so she doesn't crash?"

At that moment, I would have agreed to everything my sister asked of me. I was ready to do anything for her.

Would it be possible to find the cursed book in that utter darkness? I tried to get used to the shadows and only barely managed to make out the frames of the bookcases: they looked like black skeletons.

"We need to move forward," I said suddenly.

I squeezed Carmen's hand too hard because she protested, "Take care of me, but don't squash me."

We took a few steps forward. I could make out the bookcases and was able to walk between them, but I didn't know what direction we were going in.

As we moved farther into the room, I breathed the pleasant smell of the pages and started to feel calmer. It didn't smell stale or closed up; it smelled of papers that were put away with care, of papers that were resting.

I couldn't read those books, but they had proven themselves to be my friends. My great-grandfather and my great-uncle had read them. I remembered, also, that some of the best readers had been blind. For them, ordinary books were treasures they could only imagine. What would it feel like to read with the tips of one's fingers? I approached a bookcase, picked up a book, opened it, and caressed that tactile alphabet. I felt a tickle and had the curious sensation that the book was reading *me*. Everyone has a different fingerprint, so perhaps for those books each reader would be unique and incomparable.

I'd imagined that I had invisible friends who got together at night, but I never thought that those friends could be books. Now I knew. Every book was sleeping until it was awakened by a reader. Within these books lives the shadow of the person who wrote it.

As I was thinking this, a bookcase moved a little.

"Don't be frightened," I told Carmen. "Sometimes the books fall to make steps . . . "

I hadn't finished my sentence when two or three books fell to the floor. Then another fell, and yet another.

The books began to plummet to the floor. Since I'd already been there, I knew that they were falling with a fixed aim and that theirs was a rather orderly collapse. The books formed steps and I obeyed them. I stepped onto the first book very carefully, but then I sensed that the books were in a hurry and I started walking faster and faster, without letting go of Carmen.

It was very strange to step into the air knowing that a new step would rise to support that foot. The steps took shape as we climbed them.

We climbed until we felt a slight breeze. We were very close to the ceiling. I saw the narrow tunnel I had used before and the gap where it opened out. A sliver of moon floated in the sky.

I prepared to leave through the tunnel with the help of the staircase made of books. However, something worried me, as if I'd left the hot water tap running. I had forgotten the most important thing of all: to look for the Pirate Book!

I was about to go back when Carmen asked, "Is this it?"

"What?" I turned to look at her.

"Look—the last step. It's a book with a blue cover!" She pointed at a book illuminated by the moonlight shining through the tunnel's gap.

The books had led us up to there in the company of their rival, as if they were begging us to take it away. We had to do so.

I sat on the edge of the tunnel that led to the window and tried to pick up the book. It was very heavy, and I asked Carmen for help. Between the two of us we tugged on the book's cover. With a great effort, we managed to move it.

Little by little it grew lighter and lighter. When we reached the edge of the window, it weighed as much as a normal book. I carried it down the ladder that led to the garden.

Carmen followed me.

We had spent more time among the Shadow Books than I had thought. The moon dissolved above us and the day began to dawn. The sky turned pink with clear blue streaks.

We had done it! We had gotten that useless book out of there. That's when Carmen exclaimed, "I forgot Juanito!"

That's how it always was with her: she forgot something, she was late, she had to go to the bathroom, or she lost a toy and wanted to go back for it. Having a sister meant having all these problems.

"And Andrés?" I asked.

"Foxes are clever," she said, showing me the stuffed animal. "Juanito is the most foolish of all my toys."

I stared at her, offended that Juanito shared my name.

"He's also my favorite! We have to go back to the Shadow Club."

"First, we need to get rid of the book," I said, to gain time.

"Where are you going to put it?"

I didn't have the slightest idea of what to do with a book that only served to injure other books, but suddenly, as if the sky had heard my thoughts, I heard the ringing of a bell.

"Listen," I said to my sister.

We listened closely: it wasn't a hand bell like what I had used in the library nor was it a church bell. It didn't sound small or large. I would say it was a medium-sized bell.

It was the bell of the garbage truck, of course!

I didn't have keys to the house, so I couldn't go out into the street by myself.

What to do?

Have you ever tried to climb a vine to get over a fence? If that seems difficult, now try doing it with a large book tied to your back. Because that's what I did.

Carmen came up with the idea. She took off the sweater she always slept in (when she didn't she would dream she was at the North Pole) and used it to bind the book to my back. I've already mentioned that it weighed less now that we were out in the open. It seemed to want to flee and that's why it became lighter. Still, it is not at all comfortable to lug a bulky lump while you're trying to make your way up a vine.

The bell sounded again, this time much closer than before. I knew that the garbage truck stopped on each corner for a while. During that time, a man with very dirty yellow gloves went up and down the street, letting people know the truck was there.

I had some ten or fifteen minutes to scale the fence, jump onto the street, and run to the garbage truck.

I got stuck in the branches. I felt one of them catch my ankle. The branches bent and wrapped around my feet. Maybe Uncle had cultivated a special kind of vine to keep thieves from climbing the fence.

I was going to give up when something pushed me from behind. It wasn't a strong push; it was a small nudge of help. I spotted a branch above me and grabbed on tight. The plant wrapped itself around my wrist. That helped me lift myself up. Then I realized how to climb; if I used my feet, trying to treat the vines like a staircase, it pulled me down, but if I used my hands, I could make my way up along those loops and curls.

In the stories of the Heart-Shaped River, I learned that nature has its own rules—its own special ways of being understood. I had been using the wrong system to climb a vine but had at last discovered the right one.

I should also say something that has not ceased to surprise me after all these years: I think the evil book helped me. That little nudge I felt on my back came from it, as if it were trying to encourage me. Once I realized that, I knew what I had to do.

The Blue Book wanted to escape the house as much as I wanted to get rid of it. Although we were enemies, for a moment we both wanted the same thing and were in agreement. We were allies to reach the top of the fence; after that we would again be rivals.

When I finally got to the top, the bell had stopped ringing.

My efforts had been in vain! I had taken too long to get over the fence.

Or at least that's what I thought when I first looked out at the empty street. But then I heard the sound of an engine and saw headlights in the distance. The truck was traveling down the street toward me!

I waited for it to get closer, so close that I could smell its stench of rotten oranges, and then threw the book with all my strength. It fell among the garbage bags.

I watched it disappear down the street.

I don't know if that was the best solution. But in any case, my adversary would have few possibilities to damage other books traveling among orange rinds and other useless things.

The book wanted to save itself and to do so had helped me climb the fence, of that I'm certain. Perhaps from now on it would live as a vagabond, without coming into contact with the pages of other books that it so yearned to ruin. It seemed a sad life for it, the life of a beggar book, but at least it had saved its skin. That thought reminded me of its skin-like pages, and I was doubly glad that it was now far away from us.

It took only an instant to get back down the wall it had taken me such effort to climb. Carmen was waiting for me with expectant eyes. She hadn't taken her eyes off the wall the whole time. That's why she hadn't noticed a strange apparition in the garden: Juanito was in the grass behind my sister.

How had he gotten there? Carmen had always maintained that the hair of her stuffed animals grew, that they spoke a language we didn't understand, that they got married to one another, and had little stuffed-animal babies. In other words, she was sure they had a life of their own.

Even she, however, was surprised that Juanito got there on his own.

"What happened?" she asked me. "Did Juanito fly here?"

The only explanation I could think of is that we'd forgotten Juanito, but the books hadn't. They had helped him leave. How? We hardly know. The Shadow Books work without being seen.

Another possible explanation is that Juanito had arrived all on his own. The things we care for gravitate toward us. Everything seems to indicate that that's how things work.

Carmen hugged me and the sun flooded the garden with light as the birds started to sing—as if they all knew that we were happy.

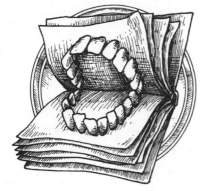

Juicier Bait

Over the course of this story I've spoken both well and poorly of my uncle. By my count, I've said eight positive and three negative things about him. From the start, I promised to be sincere. That's why I've said such disagreeable things about someone who treats me with so much affection. Now I must confess something even more difficult. I'll just say it plainly: Uncle was becoming manic about his meals.

At first, I was struck by his mixing of stories with recipes. Then I loved that his inventions were so delicious. It was also good to see him so busy and in such a good mood.

However, when he became a specialist in the kitchen, he became so immersed in his cooking that he couldn't talk about anything else. He could spend half an hour discussing pepper or mayonnaise.

If at first he used his library to make dishes inspired by stories, now he spoke of the vegetables as if they were literary masterpieces: he referred to the celery as if it were a passionate character and to the tomatoes as if they were the protagonists of an adventure novel.

Uncle had let his interests become excessive. First, the Blue Book had changed his character, and now, the kitchen held him prisoner.

Carmen, who at first had helped him happily, grew bored with Uncle and his lectures on spinach.

I must admit that his dishes were increasingly original and tasty. Uncle Tito had become an expert. Less enjoyable, though, was that he spoke like one. Nothing is more boring than knowing a lot about very little. Eventually, it became almost impossible to talk to Uncle Tito. In order to speak to him, one had to know a lot about garlic.

Those were difficult days. Catalina and I went through the section "Motors That Make No Noise" again and again, placing books there that might interest the one we wanted to find. We had rid ourselves of the Blue Book: *The Wild Book* could now move with greater freedom. But that didn't seem to have been enough. Just because you get rid of a shark it doesn't mean the other fish will approach you.

Our prey had shown curiosity, like a trout that rises toward the surface, but we still hadn't discovered the right bait.

During the long periods that we waited for something to happen as if we were fishing in a pond of still water, I thought a lot about my mother.

I hadn't seen her for many days and I was afraid I would forget what she looked like. I'd made the mistake of not bringing a photo of her to Uncle's house. The only one he had was from a long time ago, when she had fallen asleep in that field. Sometimes I tried to remember her features in detail and I felt that something didn't fit, as if the weeks of separation had been a terrible, rubber eraser. I knew that she had brown hair and eyes, that her nose was straight, and that her laughter was the most marvelous one that existed, but I couldn't picture all that in her absence.

Uncle had turned into a mad cook and I was forgetting my mother's face!

On top of everything, I began to lose faith that we'd ever find *The Wild Book*, but was afraid Catalina would realize and give up our search. If she did, she wouldn't come back to the library.

Until that moment I hadn't dared to tell her that I was in love with her because I was afraid she would find that ridiculous and would stop coming to Uncle's house. I would rather be her shadow than be rejected as her boyfriend.

Uncle Tito, Carmen, Eufrosia, and even the cats seemed to have figured out that I really liked her, but I didn't dare take the next step. What a terrible situation!

This made my spirits droop. I wanted to be someone confident, a person who didn't make mistakes, but I didn't know what to do.

Luckily, when I was at my most desperate, Catalina found a solution. She explained to me what had happened: in searching for bait for *The Wild Book*, we had acted just like Uncle in the kitchen. We chose books for experts, books that only spoke of other books.

"*The Wild Book* wants something that's more fun," Catalina suggested. "If we only offer it books about books, it's going to think that we want to classify it. It's been hidden for a long time and I don't think it wants to be a boring reference book. We should show it that letting itself be read can be a very fun adventure."

"That's true, but what book might it like?"

"You know what I think?" Catalina's honey-colored eyes shone like they did every time she had an important idea.

I was so anxious to hear her plan that I couldn't even answer. She said, "If this book is going to live among us, we must offer it something more tempting."

"Like what?"

"Something that we like! We should show it what we like so that it really gets to know us."

"Of course, like the stories of the Heart-Shaped River."

"And if it doesn't like them?" Catalina asked, suddenly worried.

I tried to encourage her. "It must know us as we truly are. If it doesn't like what we like the most, maybe it shouldn't be among us."

"You're right."

That's how we decided to place various episodes of the Heart-Shaped River in places where we thought *The Wild Book* might be.

Would it like them as much as we did? Confessing to it what sort of readers we were was the most honest thing we could do.

The stories of the Heart-Shaped River had been modified by the reading we'd done of them, so that they had the original story, but also what we had put in them. If *The Wild Book* wanted to know if we could be its friends, this was the best introduction of ourselves we could offer.

We left the bait and went to the kitchen, where Uncle wanted to talk about peanut shells. That made us certain that we'd made the right decision regarding *The Wild Book*. For days and days, we'd brought it books that made it see us as specialists in very serious subjects. Now it would know that we were also interested in stories as varied and exciting as life itself.

What happened the next day was encouraging but strange.

We walked through the section "Motors That Make No Noise" until we noticed an odd vibration. Once more, something seemed about to explode in that room.

That was when, beside *A Discovery on the Heart-Shaped River*, we saw a glimpse of paper, a white spine, without letters, a book that seemed almost finished, but that wasn't yet printed.

It peeked down at us from one of the upper shelves—the most difficult shelves to reach.

I got down on my hands and knees so that Catalina might climb onto my back, but it was useless.

A second later the book had disappeared.

The fish had approached the bait, but it didn't bite the hook.

What Starts When Something Ends

O ne day—when Uncle Tito connected the phone because he wanted to speak to a curry seller in India—we got a call from my mother.

"You've only got five more days in your uncle's house," she told me.

It seemed wonderful that we would see her again, but the news filled me with concern. Would we manage to find *The Wild Book* before my departure? What would happen with Catalina?

With a firm voice, Mama added that Papa was coming back. He would live in another house, but we would all keep seeing one another.

"Your father and I are on good terms and we love you very much."

Adults were experts at using words that could mean many different things. "Good terms" was a truly strange expression. Did it mean that he wouldn't sleep in the house but would sometimes knock on our door with a smile?

I was glad to see my mother again. I loved her so much that I wanted to remember her as she was and I was afraid I was forgetting her features. However, as soon as she mentioned that she would be coming for us, it was as if a clock I had inside me had suddenly picked up its pace.

I liked that Mama still appeared to be in a good mood these past days, but I had my own matters to resolve. I had only five days to find *The Wild Book* and to make Catalina fall in love with me. For the first time, these two things seemed inseparable.

I hung up the phone, so lost in my own thoughts that I didn't notice someone was standing beside me. It was Uncle. He looked at the floor with great sadness. "I'm going to miss you, Nephew. We only have five more days left," he added, holding up the fingers of one hand. "Will you come back and visit me?" he asked nervously.

"Of course," I answered.

"Your mother said that you'll be moving. I hope it's not too far," he added, resigned.

The city was growing at a tremendous rate. Uncle's home was in the center and it would be terrible if we moved far away, to the city's outskirts. I didn't want to keep thinking about my new house, which, with my lousy luck, would surely be on Saturn.

Uncle Tito disconnected the phone once more and we went down to the kitchen. He was so affected by the news of our departure that he didn't talk about food: he asked Carmen things about the life of her animals, proving that he had been listening to her even as he spoke of creams and stews.

"I decided to let Eufrosia cook today." He turned to look at the clock on the wall and exclaimed, "It's ten o'clock and Catalina hasn't arrived!"

I felt a hollow in my stomach and went to the pharmacy.

I found her behind the counter, busier than ever.

She explained to me that some schools had already started classes and that the students had passed around the viruses and bacteria they'd caught on their vacations. She had to help her parents.

"I can't go to the library," she said coldly.

She almost seemed more annoyed than busy.

Her mother treated me with her usual kindness, asking about my sister, my mother and my uncle. Then she told me that her daughter looked a little tired.

If she looked tired, then why was she making her work? It was Catalina who wanted to be there. Had she gotten bored of the library? Or worse—had she gotten bored of me?

I watched her as she worked with her wonderful efficiency. After a while, I dared venture the terrible question: "What's the matter with you?"

Catalina looked as if I were bothering her, but she answered like we all tend to do when we're upset and don't want to admit it. She blew a lock of hair out of her face and said, "With me?"

I thought of responding with, "Of course, with you! Who do you think I'm talking to?" But her tone had been scathing, and I was afraid of offending her. I wanted her to be pleased with me, whatever it took. I couldn't think of anything else to ask her than, "Did I do something wrong?"

I would have taken the blame for anything; I would have begged her to forgive me for the strangest things, even things like shipwrecks and wars that I had nothing to do with. I only wanted to make her smile like before.

"Don't worry," she said in an indifferent tone that nearly killed me.

"What's the matter with you!" I shouted, losing control.

"You want me to tell you?" Catalina's precious eyes looked at me in a horrible way.

"Yes," I answered, as if I were being tortured.

"Do you see this prescription?" She showed me a paper that a customer had given her.

"Yes," I answered, still in torment.

"In the pharmacy, I can find the rarest of medicines easily. I got tired of searching for a book that never appears."

"We were about to find it!"

"I don't believe so."

"You were the one who decided to offer it the books about the Heart-Shaped River. It was a good idea."

"It only made the book play hide-and-seek with us. Here my work is useful, Juan."

Although what she was saying wasn't very good, I liked that she used my name.

Ever since she was little, Catalina had worked with her parents during her summer break. She was used to the busyness of the pharmacy, and she liked to help people who needed remedies. I had never worked and couldn't imagine what it was like, but I tried to do so for the first time that difficult morning.

"That's fine," I said to Catalina.

Should I have added something more? Told her that I would be in the house for only another five days and that I needed her help to find the book?

I figured if she didn't want to help me for fun, there was no way she'd come out of pity.

I turned my back on her and walked toward the door.

Catalina caught up to me before I'd left. "Keep looking for the book on your own. I'm sure you'll find it."

Right then, I realized the difference between Catalina and me: she had a place she missed if she spent a lot of time in the library; I, on the other hand, had only the library.

I crossed the street with my head hung so low I was almost run over by a taxi. I went into my uncle's house without looking back.

I decided to find the book so that I could prove to Catalina that I was capable of doing something decisive without her help. Besides, I had nothing else to do during the brief time I had left in the house.

"Do you want me to help you, Nephew?" Uncle approached with a notebook, ready to jot down the titles of the books as he looked through them.

He had been so kind to me that I couldn't turn down his offer.

We went through the section "Motors That Make No Noise" thoroughly, but our search yielded no results other than a cramp in my right leg and a storm of sneezes from Uncle's nose—he was no longer used to the books' dust.

Disappointed, Uncle said, "I'm no Lector Princeps. The books know it. Two are needed for this search, but I'm not a good partner for you."

With those words, he gave up.

That afternoon, I wasn't in the mood to keep searching. I went to the section "The Fisherman and His Hook" and a title caught my attention: *The Mysteries of Paris*. It was strange that it was in that area of the library, but I had already grown used to the capricious leaps the books made.

When my summer vacation had started, I hated Paris because my father had gone there without us. Then, when Papa spoke to me and told me about the bridge he was building and how much he missed me, it started to seem less like an evil place. Now, seeing this book, it began to interest me.

I went back to my room, opened the book, and started to read. It told many stories at the same time—stories of people who had been tremendously wicked or tremendously good. Everything was immensely complicated there, which was perfect for someone overwhelmed by his own problems. Paris seemed like a tangle of conflicts that could make me forget my own.

As night fell I understood why this passionate book was in the section "The Fisherman and His Hook." It was my bait and it had caught me. Thanks to it, I had survived a day that had seemed unbearable.

I didn't stop reading all night long.

The first light of day found me still reading in my room. I slept for a few hours, then went downstairs for some cookies and came back to keep reading in bed. I didn't do anything else all day long.

Even while I was lost in these stories of others, I couldn't stop thinking of Catalina. People went to her pharmacy to look for remedies for illnesses—the only remedy that interested me there was Catalina herself. Since she couldn't be with me, the medicine for her absence was to travel to another world by reading thrilling stories that captivated me, but even then I always wound up thinking about her again. It was like finding myself in a labyrinth, a thrilling one, but in the end still a labyrinth. When I closed the book, I felt like I knew Paris better than my father did.

Uncle visited me in my room. He looked sad, as if he had arrived for my funeral.

"You haven't gotten out of bed. Are you feeling OK?" he asked, worried.

"I feel better," I told him, and it was the truth.

People take to their beds to recover from an illness. That's what I did, and my medicine was reading.

The next morning, a miracle happened. Well, something that seemed to be a miracle to me: Catalina rang the doorbell.

"Why didn't you tell me?" was the first thing she said.

"Tell you what?"

"That your mother is going to come for you."

"How did you find out?"

"Carmen came to the pharmacy."

I turned to look at my sister and she explained, "It wasn't my idea, it was Juanito's. He's foolish but sometimes he has good ideas. Maybe Andrés spoke to him."

Carmen had told her how we got the Blue Book out of the house. Catalina was very impressed by what we had done and that we hadn't boasted of it.

"We need to find *The Wild Book*," she said, "there's no time to lose."

225

I loved her new, resolute attitude. I was so excited that on entering the section "Motors That Make No Noise," I gave her a kiss.

I felt her smooth skin, felt a sweet and wonderful scent, felt an emptiness in my stomach, felt a tickle in the soles of my feet, felt that I traveled to the stars, felt I was floating, felt my heart and my blood and knew that I had left my body and that doing so had allowed me to feel everything more strongly. Isn't that a lot to feel after a kiss? It was, and I was enchanted.

Catalina's skin tasted of anise. No, it tasted of something better, perhaps of the mere suggestion of an anise drop. In any event, it tasted like something wonderful I'd never tasted before—it tasted of skin. I couldn't keep analyzing my feelings because a book suddenly fell on my head.

Was it chance or was it a sign? Were the books reacting to what I had done? Should I give Catalina another kiss to see?

While I was wondering about this, she headed into the depths of the room. I remained where I was, without looking at any book, completely happy that Catalina was with me and had given up her day at the pharmacy, where she could see so many people and find out everything that was going on in the city.

Libraries are isolated places and one can feel alone in them. How fun it would be to be in a place that was half-library and half-pharmacy! A place where one could chat, find out what was going on in the city, and read at the same time. A place where imagination was a part of reality. A place with remedies for illnesses that are cured with pills and for illnesses that are cured with books.

Then I remembered something. The first time that *The Wild Book* approached us, Eufrosia, Carmen, Uncle, and the cats were all in the room. Perhaps the book approached us because it felt surrounded by life; it felt that we wouldn't leave it alone and that we might adopt it.

But afterwards we did nothing but send it signs with books. It was curious about the stories of the Heart-Shaped River, but that wasn't enough.

We had to let it know that it was one of us—that it didn't just form part of the library, but that it was home, with its family.

I ran to Catalina and told her what I was thinking without pausing for breath. I almost choked.

"I didn't know you could say so many words so quickly," she said, and I saw my favorite tooth, slightly overlapping the one beside it. "What can we do?" she asked.

"Welcome it to the house. Wait for me here."

I ran to the door and saw the book that had fallen on me when I kissed Catalina. It was called *The Man Who Slept*. That book had wanted to wake me up.

Now we had to wake up *The Wild Book*.

Carmen came to the room loaded with her toys; Eufrosia came in a foul mood because she had left some darning undone; Uncle arrived full of curiosity; and Domino, Ivory, and Obsidian were happily lured in with a cup of cronopios.

I asked them all to accompany us while Catalina and I looked for the book. We weren't there to catch it, but instead to invite it to live with us.

A handful of times we thought we saw its white spine, but we didn't manage to reach it. Perhaps it was an illusion of our tired and eager eyes.

The day ended with sandwiches quickly put together by Eufrosia that, to be completely honest, weren't very tasty.

The cook was in a lousy mood. She didn't like to spend hours and hours surrounded by books she didn't want to read. Perhaps her bad mood was keeping *The Wild Book* away. I decided to modify our tactic. I asked Eufrosia to bring clothes to darn with her and asked Uncle to make a stew there among the books. We had to live as we did when we were happiest—this way the book would get to know us better.

Uncle had said that Catalina and I were Lectors Princeps. I think we were really just normal readers who were very eager to find a book we liked. We would've done anything to find that story.

While Carmen played with her animals, Eufrosia sewed tears in clothes, and Uncle kneaded a pizza in the shape of a clock, Catalina and I scanned the shelves.

Sometimes we held hands and I caressed her hair. The awaited moment came when she gave me a kiss. Then

I learned that sometimes two miracles occur simultaneously. I felt Catalina's smooth lips just as Carmen shouted, "The white book!"

We went to the area of the room where she was playing.

"I didn't see it," Carmen said. "My rabbit saw it. He has good eyesight. Besides, he is president of all the animals."

"Where is the book?" I asked her.

"So, you *do* believe that the toys are alive?"

"Does this have something to do with the book?"

"Do you think my rabbit has very good eyesight?"

"Your rabbit has excellent vision."

"On the third shelf, right in the corner. My rabbit's been looking at it for a while now," Carmen said.

I searched the third shelf.

There it was.

I felt Catalina's breath on the nape of my neck, like a gentle breeze, and moved toward the book.

This time it didn't resist. I touched the rough paper, touched its pages, held it; it was light and dense, a compact, pleasant book.

Uncle Tito, Eufrosia, Carmen, and the cats gathered around us. Catalina opened the book.

The pages were blank! All our efforts had been for nothing!

I looked up at the ceiling, which was also blank. *The Wild Book* was an empty book.

Then we felt a vibration, like that of an engine starting. The book trembled. It seemed as if the pages were feeling ticklish. They weren't used to having eyes roam all over them.

Then the book seemed to calm down, like a cat when one pets its side—although we'd only rubbed it with our eyes, wanting to read its story.

There were its pages, white as milk or snow. Did it make sense to have struggled so much to find an adventure without letters, a story without words, a blank story?

What should we do? Shake it or squeeze it until it spat out its message at last, if it even had one?

Catalina ran her fingers over the pages, as if she wanted to read it as the blind do.

"Wait a little," Uncle said, his voice broken with emotion.

And just like that, because we wanted it so badly, letters started taking shape, not little by little, but all at once. The book was now written, but it needed us to be its allies so that it could reveal itself.

The Wild Book had traveled for years without showing its story and had at last decided to abandon its solitary life.

It had found its home.

I'll never forget the days I spent in the house of my Uncle Tito, nor will I forget the adventures that led us to find this so-special book. From that moment on, I would continue to read books as if I had caught them and they were revealing their words only to me.

The day after our discovery, Mama came to Uncle's house to get us.

Seeing her was extraordinary. Not only did I recover the face that I had feared would disappear from my memory, but I also felt very light, as if until then I had carried a heavy weight which I could finally let go of.

My beloved uncle was overcome with emotion at our farewell, and he gave me some cronopios for the road. He was also glad to know that our new house wasn't far from his.

Before we left, he said something unexpected. "I've learned a lot during your visit, my dear nephew. Now I even feel the urge to go out into the street! Books improve if they are surrounded by life—that's what you've shown me. I'll come and visit you, but don't worry about catering to my particularities: I'll bring my own smoky tea. I'll travel on the bus even if the other passengers have dandruff. I've broken through the shell of my loneliness! I feel like a newborn, like an enlightened chick. I've got gray hair instead of feathers, but no chicken is perfect."

Uncle continued to be the strangest and nicest relative I had.

Then he gave me *The Wild Book*.

"It's yours," he said.

Many years have passed since this story happened, but I haven't been able to forget it. Nor did I ever forget Catalina. She kept working in the pharmacy until she was old enough to marry me.

My parents lived their lives separately, but I didn't stop seeing either of them.

During my moments of anxiety and whenever I feel lonely, books are my companions. Since that summer, books have been with me through the good times and the bad.

At last, I've told the story that I'd been keeping a secret. But I've almost taken off without revealing what *The Wild Book* was about!

Let's take a brief pause, a deep breath, and, if necessary, let's eat a cookie to recharge our strength.

Very well, we can continue.

That unforgettable day, Catalina, Eufrosia, Carmen, Uncle, the cats, the stuffed animals, and I stared at the blank pages until the book decided to show the adventures that were written in it.

The Wild Book began as follows: *I'm going to describe what happened when I was thirteen. It's something I haven't been able to forget, as if the story had me by the throat . . .*

Yes, *The Wild Book* begins just like this book does, but each reader will add something different to it.

You've read the adventure I lived through to get the book you have in your hand.

What happens next is up to you.

About the Author and Translator

Juan Villoro is Mexico's most prolific, prize-winning author, playwright, journalist, and screenwriter. His books have been translated into multiple languages. Several of his books have appeared in English, including his celebrated 2016 essay collection on soccer brought out by Restless Books, *God Is Round*. Villoro lives in Mexico City and is a visiting lecturer at Yale and Princeton universities.

Lawrence Schimel (New York, 1971) is a full-time author, writing in both Spanish and English, who has published over one hundred books in a wide range of genres. He is also a prolific literary translator. His picture books have been selected for the White Ravens from the International Youth Library in Munich, Germany and have twice been chosen for IBBY's Outstanding Books for Young People with Disabilities, among many other awards, honors, and distinctions. His work has been published in Basque, Catalan, Chinese, Croatian, Czech, Dutch, English, Esperanto, Estonian, Finnish, French, Galician, German, Greek, Hungarian, Icelandic, Indonesian, Italian, Japanese, Korean, Maltese, Polish, Portuguese, Romanian, Russian, Serbian, Slovak, Slovene, Spanish, Turkish, and Ukrainian translations. He started the Spain chapter of the Society of Children's Book Writers and illustrators and served as its Regional Advisor for five years. He also coordinated the International SCBWI Conference in Madrid and the first two SCBWI-Bologna Book Fair conferences. He lives in Madrid, Spain.

Introducing Yonder

RESTLESS BOOKS FOR YOUNG READERS

Yonder is a new imprint from Restless Books devoted to bringing the wealth of great stories from around the globe to English-reading children, middle-graders, and young adults. Books from other countries, cultures, viewpoints, and storytelling traditions can open up a universe of possibility, and the wider our view, the more powerfully books enrich and expand us. In an increasingly complex, globalized world, stories are potent vehicles of empathy. We believe it is essential to teach our kids to place themselves in the shoes of others beyond their communities, and instill in them a lifelong curiosity about the world and their place in it. Through publishing a diverse array of transporting stories, Yonder nurtures the next generation of savvy global citizens and lifelong readers.

Discover more at www.restlessbooks.com/yonder.